50 SHADES OF ORC

A MONSTER ROMANCE

L.A. MONTEIRO

CHAOS ELF PUBLISHING

Content Warning

This book contains MF open-door sex scenes with non human characters, and some light BDSM (bondage, domination, sadism and masochism).

If you're not sure what that means you're probably reading the wrong book.

CONTENTS

CHAPTER ONE

SUMMER

I wipe my wet palms nervously on my dress. The concrete high-rise at my back feels comfortingly solid in this empty alleyway, and cool compared to Sydney's heat. Up above, storm clouds darken the morning sky. They've been threatening but haven't broken yet. I know I can't stay here all day. In my ear symphonic viking metal blasts.

I've picked music fast enough to cover the beating of my heart, and to give me a pre-emptive sense of victory, but it's not doing anything for the sweaty palms. I can blame it on the humidity today, but I know my anxiety signs well enough, despite taking my pill this morning.

My parents would tell me to play something soothing, to calm my nerves. With my anxiety issues, I'm not supposed to have too much excitement. But then they weren't happy about me coming to the city at all. If I had listened to them, I'd be working for my dad's hardware store selling paint to country farmers for the rest of my life.

This is what adventure looks, and sounds like. The music crescendos, and it gives me the push I need to take another step out of the alleyway and charge down the street towards the next corner. Just one more turn and I'll see the building I'm heading to - the Orc Rights Association.

I'm in the big city now, far from home, with my dream job, or as close to it as I could get, and there's nothing that can stand in my way. *Not even Steve,* a tiny voice in the back of my head pipes up. It almost makes me falter, but another surge in the music spurs me on. Steve was a mistake, and everyone's entitled to one.

I pick up the pace, enjoying the feel of the air on my calves. The strappy summer dress and commute-efficient backpack I'm wearing make me look younger than I am, and I'm wearing my long dark hair down despite the heat. Hopefully, I'll seem like the intern they're expecting.

I'd better look right, or I'm out of a job. I push the thought aside, along with Steve, and focus on taking the next step, around the corner, to my destiny.

An angry mob surrounds the building. The guitar solo in my ears suddenly feels jarringly out of place. I pull my headphones off.

"Say no to orcs!" one protestor screams, facing the rest of the crowd from the doors I've been heading for. She's older than I am - in her early 30s at least, with mousy brown hair and a gray hoodie. She looks a lot more like the intern I'm pretending to be, but she's holding up a sign with a cartoon green face crossed out. Around her are about ten people, some holding signs, some handing out pamphlets. A few interested spectators surround the protest, spectating the show.

"Say no to orcs," some protestors echo.

"Orcs don't belong here!" the woman shouts. "They're murderers and rapists."

I wonder which orcs the woman is talking about. Most of the 200 orc refugees who abruptly appeared on a busy Sydney street five years ago ended up in the military or in private armies, and the rest lived on the streets. Every incident involving orcs is carefully monitored, and rape has never been reported.

"Focus on the story," my editor would say.

"Stay calm," my parents would say.

Maybe they're both right. I breathe in. An oily feeling comes from the crowd - it's a sensation I've felt before, and learned not to ignore, but also not to talk about. The crowd has bad intentions. My feelings about people are rarely wrong, and often useful, but sometimes they come with unwanted side effects.

I breathe out.

I put my headphones back on, hit play, and push my way through the crowd, head down.

A camera light flashes. *Shit!*

My eyes scan the crowd - protestors surround me, and I'm almost in front of the scowling woman. There's not a camera in sight.

If any of the other press have seen me, my cover is on a ticking clock. I have a small social media following from my university days, and I didn't think to take my photo down before this undercover gig. It's supposed to be in and out of here quickly, gathering whatever intel I need.

If I blow my cover without getting anything, I might be out of a job. Every journalist needs a big story in their first few months to prove themselves, and I haven't had mine yet. She hasn't said anything but I can tell my editor is worried.

It's going to be okay. Viking metal is in my ear and I'm too close to give up now.

I press on, past the scowling woman and towards the door.

It shouldn't surprise me when she stands in front of me. She says something and I pull my headphones down.

"Are you going in there?" the woman asks angrily. The oily feeling is directional now - coming from this woman.

"Er...yes?" I say. I look past her and step to the side. She steps in front of me again.

My hands curl into fists as a wave of anger surges up inside me. I could push this woman and she would be on the floor. I could punch her, and she would bleed at my feet.

My heart beats staccato in my chest as visions of violence flash in my mind.

A memory of my mother's worried face cuts through.

I breathe in. I breathe out.

I'm so hot I could be on fire, but at least I can feel my skin again. I focus on pushing the anger down. My fists relax.

"Can I help you?" a smooth voice asks from behind the woman. A man in an expensive gray suit has a flat hand out towards me and the other on the open door to the building.

He pointedly ignores the obnoxious protester, but she's unsurprisingly silent, staring at him in shock.

She's not the only one.

There's no mistaking Tom Johnson, billionaire. And to top things off, standing beyond him in the building is the only female orc on Earth. Her name comes to mind from a million news articles - Olivia. Looking elegant in a darker gray suit, a security wire in her ear. She's very tall, and her muscles bulge through her shirt. She frowns at the crowd.

It's then I realize the protestors behind me are quieter than they were a moment ago. I was so busy controlling my own emotional state, I didn't notice the shift in the air.

Tom raises his eyebrows at me in question.

Perfect cheekbones, designer haircut, designer suit. In some ways, he could have walked straight out of a picture. And I've seen plenty of them - Tom on the red carpet, dating some actress, Tom on the cover of Billionaire magazine.

What the pictures don't show is the intensity in his eyes. They're dark brown, almost black. They glimmer with intelligence. His brow is more furrowed than it looked in the photos, giving him the sense of a predator tracking his prey. There's a tension in his jaw too - this is a man ready to pounce.

There's a story in him - I can feel it. The violence surging through me a moment ago pauses. I'm tracking a different kind of prey now.

He's looking straight at me. His eyes widen slightly. He's noticed I'm staring.

I reach for his hand, and he leads me inside in two steps. His bodyguard steps in behind us and shuts the door.

The magic hush from outside seems to be broken by the glass barrier between the orc and the protestors, as the chanting outside starts up again. Olivia huffs a laugh.

We're in a small reception area, too small to be called a waiting room. There's a desk with nobody behind it.

A corridor to our right seems to lead to more offices, and a lift sits closed on the left-hand wall.

A flustered-looking man with a bald spot and a crumpled gray suit emerges from the corridor. "Oh, Mr Johnson and Olivia, I'm so sorry about this. Please come through." The man turns to me. "And I don't believe we've met?"

Clammy hands make a comeback as I sweat my way through the lie. "Um, I'm Summer? The intern?"

The man's face clears. "Oh, of course. I'm Professor Houston," the man says. "So glad to have you. And I'm so sorry for the hubbub outside. They do crop up now and then, but they're mostly harmless."

"Thanks so much for taking me on," I say awkwardly, then turn back to Tom. "And thank you for the rescue back there..." My smile falters.

Tom's gaze is sliding down my body, subtly assessing me.

A hot wave runs through me, and I feel my cheeks heat up.

It's not embarrassment. It's like the anger from outside and pursuit of the story have rolled into something new, making my heart pump faster and my body sit up and pay attention.

It's not attraction. He's as handsome in real life as the magazines say, but it's not like I'm a virgin and I've never had this kind of physical reaction to a man I've barely spoken to.

It's the adrenaline my mother always warned me could trigger my anxiety. She somehow didn't consider a scenario where a billionaire I'm trying to dig up dirt on is checking me out.

When he looks back up into my eyes, he appears slightly embarrassed, which is the only thing that stops my newfound emotional turmoil from switching to rage. Instead, my body twitches restlessly, like it's screaming at me to wake up, and I consciously take a breath to calm down.

He's still watching me, which doesn't help.

'No problem," the orc woman says with a pleasant voice, breaking our bizarre stand off.

I turn to her, grateful to look away, and my internal rollercoaster takes another turn. I've never seen an orc in real life before. Not to mention a woman.

The orc is taller than any human, with dark green skin and long black braided hair falling down her back. Apart from the coloring and the slight ridges at her brow, she's nearly human looking. She even has red nail-polish.

Small tusks jut upwards on either side of her mouth.

"Oh, no of course not - I... it's lovely to meet you," I stammer, embarrassingly. Good thing I'm undercover as an intern and nobody expects me to sound intelligent.

"The pleasure's all mine. I'm Olivia." She purrs the words, and there's a flirtatious smile to her lips. I notice a flash of irritation on Tom's face and wonder at it. Olivia takes my hand and kisses it.

Her hand feels normal-sized, and for a second, I'm distracted entirely by the press of her lips on my skin.

Then Tom cuts in. "Professor, I believe you were going to show us a presentation." His tone is cold.

Olivia smirks and winks at me. I blink, not trusting myself to say anything as I take my hand back and the professor invites me to join them.

As I follow them, my mind is whirling.

It's well known, Tom Johnson secured the services of the only female orc known on Earth and made her his personal bodyguard. It's broadly considered a genius PR move and cements his reputation as an unconventional entrepreneur.

But there are questions. Why is it Tom was the only billionaire to think of investing in the orcs? Why does he care so much he set up a facility to house half the orc population, and set up the Orc Rights Association only months ago?

And now I wonder, what is his relationship with his bodyguard? That's exactly the sort of thing I'm here to find out.

CHAPTER TWO

TOM

I tap my fingers on the table impatiently. Olivia and I are in a small meeting room. The professor and Summer are absent. He said he was getting ready - he must also be settling in the distracting intern.

The room is small but not shabby, with a decent wooden table and a screen set up for presentations. They're well-funded without too much fat - and I should know. The professor's venture is just one of my attempts at helping the orc people - my people.

I had a one year head-start on Earth before the rest of the orcs arrived. Using secret pathways known to only a few shape-changers like myself, I readied the caches of wealth left by those before me. I gathered enough to start our lives here. But my people are proud and difficult, and my fool of a brother doesn't help. And so I'm here, immersing myself in a civilized human world that makes my claws itch, to help the fool and his followers.

Olivia breaks my musing with her smirk. "How're you going there?" she asks. She taps her own fingers on the table.

She's a professional at getting under my nerves - that's what siblings do, no matter what species. I'm sure she paints her nails bright red just to bother me. They jar with the rest of her look - a dark gray suit, bodyguard's ear coil and dark green skin.

My objection isn't aesthetic but political. As the only openly free orc in this world, she's supposed to be reminding people of how civilized orcs can be, not painting her nails the color of fresh blood.

"Might I remind you; you're supposed to be my servant?" I point out. She ignores the ice in my tone.

"Bodyguard," she corrects. "They're not into servitude in this world."

"Probably why the humans show each other so little respect," I snarl.

"Sure, it's respect you were showing when you were eyeing off Summer, and not a response to the mouth-watering scent rolling off her. Pretty too. Not tempted to ask her out?"

"Women are a distraction."

"So, you won't mind if I ask her out?"

I almost growl at her to remind her who she's speaking to, but our host returns.

"I'm so sorry... Bit of pre-presentation nerves, you know," the professor says, twisting his hands together. Olivia smiles. I do not. "My new intern is just fetching us some water."

My shoulders tense, thinking of Summer coming back into the room. Damn Olivia, she's right about the girl's scent.

"So um, shall we begin?" the professor says, sitting down and adjusting his glasses as he pulls a presentation up on the screen.

Summer walks in holding three glasses of water on a tray. A strained smile is plastered on her face. She avoids everyone's eyes. As she enters, a waft of her scent flows in with her. Is it her shampoo? There's something floral to it, and something musky. It reminds me, oddly, of home.

She's not wearing the headphones anymore, or the backpack. The red dress is pretty. It makes her look free, like she could break out dancing at any moment.

"Ah, thank you Summer," the professor says. "If you please?" She puts his glass down on the table. He drinks as if he's dying of thirst while she walks towards Olivia and I with the other glasses.

She puts one in front of Olivia first, and then me. She's so close I can almost feel the heat of her skin. My nostrils flare involuntarily. Then she takes a seat across from me, with the tray on the table in front of her.

The presentation starts with the press images of dozens of male orcs looking startled and snarling on a Sydney street. They're surrounded by camera-snapping spectators. All of them are muscle-bound, with characteristic green skin and tusks, wearing rough armor and carrying spears and axes. An image I've seen hundreds of times.

"Since my new intern is joining us today, I might just start with an introduction, for her sake?" the professor looks at me in question. Olivia says, "Go ahead," before I have time to speak.

The professor clears his throat and begins with a dry tone. It's clear he's used to lecturing in classrooms. "The orcs landed in the world five years ago, refugees from a war in another dimension. They were clearly warriors, but they did no harm to the somewhat reckless Sydneysiders surrounding them when they first arrived. Only 200 in number, and 199 of them male." My fingers tap on the table again.

Olivia kicks me under the table and looks at me with a mild, interested expression on her face. The professor might not know I'm an orc - nobody does - but Olivia's identity is clear and I'm braced for him to say something offensive. She won't react, but I have no qualms in correcting him if he missteps.

"The military was the first to step in, seeing the potential of this warrior race, and the fate of the orcs was considered sealed. But then the cultural differences became apparent. Some adjusted to the military, but many did not. A year ago Mr Johnson funded a private facility outside of Sydney offering sanctuary to the orcs, and many of them are now housed there. But not all chose to live there - about half the orc population refused the facility. Some ended up in private security, others in prison, and many on the streets."

Another slide, this time of a homeless orc, head bowed and sitting on the sidewalk. Olivia's neutral expression saddens. I want to reach out and touch her shoulder, to say that I understand, but we are not brother and sister in this meeting. So I stay still and return my attention to the human.

"We were braced for another portal opening - another set of orcs to come through - or something less friendly. But the portals never reopened. And the orcs are stuck here. But what next for this stranded race?"

He takes a breath, and I assume the point of his presentation is coming. Or I'm at risk of letting my orc burst out from beneath this human skin and disembowel him with my claws.

"As you know, my background is in cultural studies, politics and sociology. With your funding, I've set my mind to the question of what the next best steps would be to ensure this race survives in this world."

The professor flicks to the next slide, which features a pregnant woman. "The most obvious issue for the race is the lack of breeding. With only one female orc, and her unable to breed..." Here the professor nods apologetically at Olivia, who smiles at him in encouragement. It doesn't bother her she can't breed; it gives her more freedom than she would have been allowed otherwise.

"Studies will have to be done to see if there are women who can bear orcish children. There are, of course, urban legends of orcs mating with women as far back as the 18th century on Earth. The women are called mystics and revered in orcish culture. But these are only legends, and there's been no proof that there really was travel between our two worlds dating that far back."

The professor is right. A lot of my money has been dedicated to genetic testing ventures and we haven't found an orcish woman so far. Without breeding, the orcs on this world have a limited lifespan. But I know all this, and I ignore Olivia's pointed look. There is no proof of the legendary mystics. We can't pin our hopes on dreams. "Let's move on from the urban legends, shall we, professor? I want to know about your new research."

"Ah, of course." The professor looks excited, and flicks to the next slide, featuring a smiling orc in a blue jumpsuit adjusting a bolt on a plane with his fingers. An equally cheerful human sits in the cockpit. "The way to make orcs function well in our society is a complex issue, and at the heart of it is reputation. The orcs come across like warriors, and our fiction of them, and their history, supports this. Sympathy towards the orcs is essential to change public perception of them. And to be seen as sympathetic, the orcs must have a champion." The professor flicks to a new slide, with a superhero in a cape on it. "A public figure who is seen as successful, admirable and good."

I completely ignore the amused look Olivia shoots me. "An orc as a hero? You think the public will ever see that?" There's bitterness as well as doubt in my voice. I know how people see us. Maybe if I were human, as the professor thinks I am, I would buy this rubbish.

Worse yet, I know why he's thinking along these lines.

"There was that incident of the orc stopping a shooting a few weeks ago..." he continues.

The incident that's been all over the news, and has been haunting me for the past two months. I cut him off abruptly. "The orc was drunk. He stopped the shooting, but it was an accident. They were shooting. He was in the way and took steps to stop them shooting again. He was no hero. Try again."

"My studies show it's the only way. And if this orc received some media training..."

"Training? Like a dog?" Heat creeps up my neck. If he knew the orc in question... "They can't be trained. I briefed you that the orc people are proud and unyielding, professor. And I pay a lot for your salary. Is this all my funding has bought? This is a waste of my time."

"I assure you..." The professor's face goes red as he flusters.

"I assure YOU that if you don't come up with something better than this, funding to this program will be cut."

"I left my tenure for this," the professor starts.

"And I left my office for this. We're leaving." Rage pulses under my skin, and I can feel my orc roar. We're leaving before I do or say something I regret. I push it aside, but know if I don't get out of here, I'll do something everyone will regret.

Ice cold water in my lap cuts short that train of thought. Summer is standing in her chair. She had stood up and pushed the tray towards me, knocking over my water glass.

I look up into Summer's flushed face, and in her eyes see a feral anger. My own anger rises in an uncontrollable rush, and I barely restrain the urge to reach out and pin her in place.

I stand and sneer instead, as the professor lets out an exclamation of "Oh my goodness!"

Olivia snorts with amusement.

Summer blinks, and a hot flush rises to her cheeks as she looks down and away from me. She appears suddenly mortified. "I'm s... so sorry," she says.

"You've done enough." There's steel in my voice but I can't stop it. Normality is beyond me now, and I have to rely on the force of will that keeps me in check in this form.

Summer seems to have come back to herself, but it's not so easy for my kind. My skin is crawling for release. I'm suddenly aware of the weight in the air, the wetness of the impending storm outside. Then I smell the jungle and hear the chirp of the native carrion birds that follow my kind when we're hunting. And that smell of her... that smell seems stronger.

I shake my head, surprised at the strength of the vision of home.

"Oh dear, I'm so sorry, Mr Johnson. Summer, could you please fetch some paper towels?" the professor frets.

"That's unnecessary, professor," Olivia smoothly intervenes, and stands beside me. For once she's supporting me, and I'm surprised. I'm not sure if she can feel whatever Summer's doing to me or just sense that I'm on the edge. In her orc form, she towers over Summer and the professor in the small room. Summer steps back when Olivia stands up. With Summer further away, I can breathe more easily.

"P... perhaps we could pay for dry cleaning?" the professor asks.

"Oh, we can afford it," Olivia says casually.

"O... of course," the professor says.

Summer is still staring at the floor. She needs to get out of the way. I'm not sure I can control myself if I have to brush past her, if she touches me. All I want to do is walk out and leave this disaster behind.

She steps back and I almost sigh with relief. I walk straight out the door and head to the lift, pressing the button to the basement.

I know Olivia called the car there as soon as we ran into the protestors. I get in and take the elevator down, leaving them all behind.

CHAPTER THREE

SUMMER

"Sorry about Mr Johnson, Professor," Olivia says when Tom leaves the room. "I know the orc in the shooting and Tom tried to help. But they're a proud race and we've run into some challenges. I wouldn't be surprised if he calls you later with an apology."

"Oh that's quite alright," says the professor. He's visibly relieved. "I'm so sorry about the water incident."

"That's not a problem. But maybe Summer can walk me to the lift and tell me more about her motivations. Shall we?" Olivia asks, and gestures me to follow her after Tom's departing back.

I look hopelessly at the professor, but he only nods at me encouragingly.

When we get into the waiting room, Tom's already taken the lift downstairs. She presses the button and we stand and watch the numbers go down.

"I'm so sorry about the accident," I stammer. My mother's worried face rises to my mind again. I should never have left home, I'm a complete failure, and I've screwed this right up.

"Oh, don't mind him, he's just easily upset," says Olivia. "Probably that time of the month or something. I hear that's something that happens to humans."

"Just women," I say. "Isn't that... I mean, in your species..." I scour my brain to remember if I've read something about this.

She laughs. "I'm joking. Our reproductive system isn't that different to humans."

"Oh," I say, embarrassed. Inside, my brain is screaming. I'm speaking to the only female orc on earth. I should ask her something that not everyone knows. But she's disarming, smirking at me as if sizing me up.

"Tom Johnson isn't in the business of insulting employees," she says. "But I know him pretty well, and I think he might like to spend more time with you. And you'll have time to impress him with something other than your waitressing skills. Can I grab your number for him?"

"My number?..." I gawp at her before snapping my mouth shut and saying, "Sure", and reciting my number to her after she pulls out her mobile from a pocket and types it in. I highly doubt Tom Johnson is going to call me, but if he does, my editor might give me a raise right then and there.

The elevator doors open. She steps in the lift and wiggles her fingers goodbye to me as the doors close.

Then I'm alone in the waiting room, wondering what just happened.

I remember walking into the room and trying not to stare at Olivia. I remember walking towards Tom and Olivia with the water. Tom's face comes back to me - tense and vicious, and his voice - whip-like as he scolded the professor. I remember my heart racing, and the feeling that Tom was dangerous - more dangerous than he should be for a business meeting. I felt he needed to be stopped.

Rage had torn through me, and I couldn't see for a second. Then it was as if someone else had pushed his glass over, like my hand had moved of its own volition.

Maybe my mum's right, maybe I should never have left home. But I hadn't had an incident for years before Steve. And now I'm back on medication, I should be completely under control. Today was an aberration.

I grab my backpack from behind the reception area where I'd stashed it and walk out the front doors. At some point it started raining hard outside, but there's a bit of cover above the front door. I could make a dash for it, but I'm not even sure where I'm going. If I leave now, my cover as an intern is probably blown. And what will that do to my meeting tonight? Unless it's a date?

No, that would be ridiculous.

That doesn't stop my heart pounding. I breathe deep and long, staring out into the rain.

When I feel calmer, I get out my phone. A message from my mother. "Don't forget you always have a place here. Love you xxx" and a picture of her and my dad being goofs. It makes my heart ache.

"Love you too," I flick back.

As far as they're concerned, things are going great for me in the big city. I've been hiding things from them for years, knowing they'd never give me the freedom I need if they knew I was still plagued with incidents like today. The only way I got through was with the support of my genius sister, Em. Genius and the sneakiest person I know. If she wasn't already destined to be a great biologist, she'd be a much better journalist than me. But as soon as she was old enough, she took off for university in Canberra, and I was left with my anxious parents and boring small town. It wasn't long after she left, I moved to Sydney.

I dial her number. She picks up on the third ring. "Em, I screwed up."

"What happened?"

"He, um... he got to me. I lost my temper. Like with Steve."

"Who did? And Steve is an asshole."

"Tom Johnson did. And Steve is just a guy who lives in a big city trying to make a living," I say. "That's what he said, anyway. When the bleeding stopped."

"He dated you, then lied to you and stole your story, Summer. You really believe that's acceptable behavior?"

"In this city? Yeah, I think I do. And if Steve is just a regular guy, so is Tom Johnson. He definitely screams big city - he's not like the boys at home at all,"

"The incredibly boring boys at home you wanted nothing to do with?" Emily jibes.

I choose to ignore that. "Anyway, he was being an asshole to this lovely professor. So, I poured water into his lap and I can't stay an intern here, so I've probably blown my cover, and then his orc bodyguard got my number for him."

"You gave the orc your number?"

"No - well yes, but for Tom Johnson."

Emily pauses. "That's awesome."

"But I was supposed to be posing as an intern to go through their files."

"Who cares about the internship? The meat to this story is Johnson himself, and if you calm down for a second, you'd remember that."

See? Genius. "Oh god, you're right."

"And are you actually fired from your fake job right now?"

"Er... I mean, I left the building. But I'm outside."

"So, you could go back in. Didn't you say the professor was lovely? He might let you back in. You only need your cover to hold for a day."

"Total genius," I say aloud this time.

"No worries, now go get em," she signs off.

The professor is sitting dejected in the room he presented in when I get back inside, flicking back through the presentation he showed earlier. It's a bit nerve-wracking approaching him. Even though I'm not the intern I claimed to be, I hate disappointing people.

"I'm so sorry, professor," I begin.

He waves my apology away and gestures me into a chair. "You've just finished a degree in sociology, yes?" I nod my head. That's what my cover story says. "I'd like your opinion on this presentation."

He goes through the whole thing. I wasn't paying that much attention last time. I could only see Tom Johnson's reaction. Most of the presentation isn't new information, but the solution is innovative and smart. Nothing that warranted Tom's rude reaction.

The slide show ends, and the professor looks at me with a question in his eyes. I shouldn't say anything - I'm an intern, he can't really be hoping I'll have an answer. And anything I say now could blow my cover. But asking questions now could help with the story - and maybe help the professor at the same time.

"I can't see anything wrong with the presentation, professor, so maybe the issue is Tom himself?"

"Go on?" the professor asks, slightly desperately.

"Well... go back two years ago and Tom Johnson was a relative unknown. He was an Australian-born tech investor who started in Silicon Valley and came back to Australia to settle down. He lives in Sydney and has kept his investment portfolio going strong. He's responsible for the dating app In Tune, that uses genetic profiling to help people find their dream match. It took off last year, and now he's a billionaire. Before now, he had no philanthropic ventures, but then he opened his orc sanctuary. Word on the street is that Tom wants to monetize the orcs, turning them into a private militia. Do you think that's true?"

He looks shocked. "Absolutely not. The media have demonized him, but I believe his heart is in the right place with this. He shot down the idea of a private militia in our first meeting."

Interesting. "But Tom Johnson doesn't contribute to any other charitable causes. How does the orc refugee cause serve him? Perhaps if you can understand that you can understand what he's looking for?"

"Summer, I think you have him wrong. He genuinely believes in orc rights. I think that bodyguard of his has swayed him to the cause," the professor says.

"I wish I could believe that," I say. Surprisingly, I mean it. "But I can't see any other clues. Do you have alternative solutions for him?"

The professor sighs. "There are no other options. Orc refugees are not an appealing charity. They are stranded in this world with no help or prospects - they're big, green and scary. Cruel people say we should just eliminate them. And even with our help, their fate is sealed without the ability to breed. We can only hope to learn as much from them as we can while they're still here, and for that people have to accept them."

I should steer him towards the admin work I could do today. I want to access his passwords, scour through his databases and see who else supports the organization. And I intend to do all that later. But for a second, he looks so sad, sitting there, that I think maybe he just needs a little hope.

I find myself saying, "Tom's bodyguard got my number for him. If he calls me, perhaps I could pick his brain further and see if there are some solutions he might be receptive to?"

When his face lights up, I have no reason to feel good, but I do.

Chapter Four

TOM

Click-Clack

Olivia's red nails thrum against the metal window frame. It's the only sound in the back seat of the limousine beyond the low hum of the engine. The privacy screen is up between us and the driver.

I stare out the window of the passenger seat into traffic. The sky overhead is a black smudge of heavy clouds.

Click-Clack

My teeth grind together. I'm waiting for all the things she's dying to say. "I don't suppose you could stop that?"

"Huh?" Olivia turns. Her red eyes open wide in a picture of innocence, but I'm not fooled for a second.

She suppresses a grin. I wonder if my eyes have turned red, and I close them, breathing deeply, willing my human skin to stay in place. I hate being smaller than her in this form.

When I open my eyes, she's watching me, eyes dancing with amusement. "Nice girl, huh? I got her number. For a dinner date."

"I hope you have a good time," I say dryly, ignoring the surge of jealousy her words bring.

"For you, idiot. She could be a mystic. I saw the sparks between the two of you - she reacted like an orc woman, and you reacted back. Plus, it might be fun. You should call her."

"That woman poured water on me. My reaction was rage."

"That's exactly the way orcs act when they're in heat. It starts as almost a blood rage."

I shift uncomfortably in my seat. She's right about the blood rage. My heart beats faster even thinking about the way Summer smelled. My mouth waters involuntarily and I swallow hard.

Mystics were shape-shifting orcish women, rare and extremely unlikely in this world. My people spent too much time hunting for mystics in this world. Orcs terrified female humans with their pursuits, and the media went into a frenzy. Women came forward claiming to be mystics, only to disappoint an already desperate orc population.

My biology division was blood testing every willing human available, and they'd found nothing for years. Admittedly, they had to work largely in secret.

"I won't waste more of our time on that myth. Mystics don't exist and chasing a fantasy is a distraction from something that might actually help our people. As head of the clan and one of the few orcs able to shift forms, I don't have the luxury of fun." My voice drips acid, hoping to shut her down but knowing it won't work.

"You don't think she smelled unusual?"

"I agree, she smelled good. Better than most. They smell like decaying flowers and plastic."

"That's the perfume and makeup the rich women use. Not all human women smell like that," she says with a cheeky and knowing grin. I resist the bait. Although I know she'd love to tell me, Olivia's personal life is her own affair.

"Could you really see that woman as a queen?" I drip derision to shut her down. There was nothing about Summer that spoke to the ferocity of an orc or the leadership our people would need from my mate. Except for a few seconds, after she poured the water on my lap. That look in her eye was enough to drive me to distraction. A distraction I don't need. "We need a better solution," I remind her, my tone still serious, but softer. "And I know you want to talk about the professor's suggestion."

She nods soberly, expression hardening up. For all her japes, my sister is a keen strategist. "It's worth considering."

"We had a plan. You stay orcish, I stay human, your gender is perceived as kinder in this world, and we can convince them through our alliance that we're civilized."

"The plan isn't working. Half of our people are on the streets, Tom." That look again - she's a warrior, but my sister bleeds inside for our people. She's too soft. That's why I can't be.

"That's because my brother is too damn stubborn to accept help." I say, slamming my hand on my thigh in frustration. The orcs who refused my sanctuary are those who listen to my brother, believing his inability to shift makes him a purer orc leader. My simple brother who thinks with his fists more than his head, and shuns the way I've built my fortune.

She waits until I'm calm. "I know they're suffering. But laws around orcish business ownership don't exist. We could lose everything we've worked for. It's an enormous risk, not to mention the fact I've been lying to this world for years. All my alliances will be in jeopardy. All the wealth we've accumulated, too."

"You hired the professor for a reason. He knows what he's talking about. We could dress up another one of the orcs. Let's assume we find one less drunk and stubborn. We could try to make him respectable, but we both know time is against us. There's an election around the corner. Public opinion is shifting against us with these protests on the rise."

She's right. The new Premier in the state is on record as believing the orcs have no place in the country and should be treated like any other refugee. The glamor and excitement of their initial existence only lasted as long as they were useful in the military. Now most of them have realized military life was too close to the slavery we knew in our old world.

"I'll think about it," I say curtly.

"We might not have a choice," Olivia says, softer now. She's being the reasonable one for a change, which is enough to make me pause. Until her next sentence.

"Speaking of no choices, I made you a reservation for Dos Capas at 6pm."

I growl audibly now. She ignores me and presses a number in her phone. She hands it to me as it rings.

"It's close to home." She doesn't say it, but that means it's also close to a large homeless orc population. Whether they stay close to me for protection or because my brother wants them to watch me, I don't know. I do know it's said that when one of the legendary mystics is around enough orcs, her true nature will break free. "If she stays human, or doesn't jump your bones, then you'll know. And if not, you've had a nice dinner. You might not believe in the mystics, but in case they exist, take this chance, Tom. You have a duty."

"Hello?" It's Summer's voice answering on the end of the line.

Olivia raises her eyebrows at me. She's stubborn as hell but she's right. I have a duty. I take the phone and use my professional voice. "Hello Summer, this is Tom Johnson. If you're interested in dining with me tonight, be at Dos Capas at 6pm. I'll be there." Then I hang up, hand the phone back to Olivia.

She frowns at me, but says nothing.

I ignore her and stare out the window, ignoring the way my heart speeds up when I think of seeing Summer again.

CHAPTER FIVE

SUMMER

Is this a date? I can't help but wonder it, even as another part of my brain cuts in and reminds me to think of the story.

I'm standing outside Dos Capas, feeling awkward and sweating. It's 6.05pm and I wonder if Tom Johnson is going to stand me up. The sky is quickly slipping from dusk to night, but at least it's not raining.

Maybe he was lying. Or maybe he wants me to be embarrassed, as revenge for pouring water on him today.

Random anxieties whirl through my mind. Usually they're not this bad, but these are exceptional circumstances. Maybe I should have taken two pills today or brought one with me. But I didn't, so I'll just have to deal with it.

It's busy enough in the restaurant, but the rest of the street is empty and industrial. This is a weird area - a mixture of gentrified restaurants, wealthy housing and homelessness.

The brick wall I'm next to is faux industrial, but it's all slick and black decor inside. I'm wearing a backless black minidress, no jacket, and no handbag. All I'm carrying is my phone in my hand. It's an outfit that says I've got nothing to hide. I get appreciative glances from passing men and the occasional woman, which is gratifying. This is my most flattering dress, and it's the best choice for this venue. It has nothing to do with wanting to knock Tom Johnson's socks off.

Thunder rolls threateningly overhead. The storm looks like it's about to break any second. The tension in the air is thick and I check my phone again. 6.07pm.

I turn randomly and start walking away from the restaurant. I've never been good at standing still and waiting around. If I go for a walk and he's not here when I get back, I'll know he's definitely stood me up.

I'm a few feet from the restaurant when a man turns a corner and stumbles into me in a cloud of sour, unwashed body smell.

He steps back and I notice how tall he is, and how broad. And then I freeze, realizing he's an orc.

This is the second orc I've ever seen in person. And judging from the scowl on his face, it's probably not going to go as well as the last one did.

He breathes stale booze breath onto me and staggers back, swearing. "I'm so sorry," I say, taking a step back. It wasn't my fault, but he looks mean and I'm not sure how else to get out of this except to go back towards the populated restaurant.

"Watch where ya going, ya bitch!" he shouts.

He towers over me, green and huge, forcing me to take a step back, up against the brick wall behind me. My phone clatters loudly as it falls to the pavement, but he's standing too close for me to bend down to get it. I can't take my attention off him. His breath is overwhelming.

Then he leers, looking down at my body. "You smell good."

Until now, I've been focused on avoiding his bad breath and trying to get back to the restaurant behind me. But now my heart beats faster, and my nails cut into my palms as I hold in the fight.

My mother's face floats in my mind, shaking her head. She was always worried that I'd have an outburst in a situation I couldn't get myself out of - do something foolish at the wrong time.

I grit my teeth and breathe in steadily. She's right. This guy's much bigger than me. If I start something with him, I could end up killed. I should get back to the restaurant and get help. Or scream for it.

He shoves me back against the wall with one big green hand. My shoulders slam back, pain jarring through me as I bash against the brick. It knocks the breath out of me, and the humidity suddenly feels suffocating.

He smiles. For some reason, I remember pouring water on Tom Johnson's lap.

I understand the meaning of the word 'seeing red,' when I'm like this. The edges of the world blur as the rage rises, and all I see is this ugly mug's face ready for my fist.

But he pushes his hand into my shoulder again, keeping me pinned in place, and his nostrils flare while he sniffs me.

He's incredibly strong. Dimly, I understand why people are afraid of orcs. But it's not fear that's making my legs shake. The entire world is full of him. Nobody is coming. A completely irrational voice in my mind says, "That means you can give him exactly what he deserves."

My fists are clenched and trembling, and he still has me pinned. It looks like I have little choice but to push back. No more control, no more reining it in. Something like relief floods me.

He looks amused when I smile. Oh, I'm going to enjoy this.

I tense my shoulders to swing when a commanding voice, laced with steel, cuts in, "That's enough."

The pressure on my shoulder suddenly releases as the orc swings around, snarling to face Tom Johnson.

"Your business is done here," Tom says with disgust.

From this angle, I can see the dog tags swinging at the orc's neck. Even without his size, he's been trained in combat in this world, and if the rumors are true, in his own world, too.

I would have been incredibly lucky to come out alive if I'd tried to tangle with this creature. But will Tom Johnson fare any better? He's not a small man, but he's a foot shorter than the formidable orc.

While he's distracted, I bend to get my phone, opening it hurriedly and dialing emergency.

"Leave before I decide to get involved," Tom says coldly, with all the arrogance of a billionaire.

My eyes must be like dinner plates, staring wildly back at the orc to see what his reaction is going to be, while the phone rings out in my ear. I wanted a story, but I wasn't expecting to cover Tom Johnson's death.

Before the phone connects, I'm shocked to see the orc stumble back, hands before him as if warding off a blow, head bowing in deference.

"Forgive me my lord, I didn't realize..." he says, before running backwards and disappearing around the corner.

As he leaves, the energy leaves my body in a rush. It's as if my strings have been cut. I slump against the wall, feeling sticky with sweat and exhausted. I look down at my phone - it's connected. Dimly, I hear someone speaking on the other line, but I don't feel in danger anymore. As I hang up, I wonder, "what did the orc mean by 'my lord'?"

"You don't look good," Tom says, appearing concerned.

"Thanks," I say weakly. It's all I have the energy to say as I pull myself together. The shock of seeing Tom in the confrontation has diffused some of my irrational rage, but not all. I'm sucking in deep breaths to calm myself.

"I don't mean that..." he says it coldly. He's far too calm after such a confrontation. His cheek twitches, the only sign his control is shaken. "You look ill and shaken up. Perhaps we could go back to my place so you can rest, and we can be somewhere less..." he looks around the street. "Somewhere safer."

I know where he lives, and he's looking roughly in that direction. It's not far. The apartments he lives in are famous for their luxury and prominent celebrity owners, and they're only a street away.

But he's inviting me back there before we've even been on a dinner date. Is he really being chivalrous, or is he trying to skip straight to dessert?

"I'm not far," he says. "You look like you could use a sit down." He looks at me coldly, and I know he's not interested in dessert - he's far too controlled for that.

"I know where it is," I say, and take a step forward, stumbling a little.

Tom reaches out to take my shoulder, and I lean into him. He smells delicious - like luxury cologne and musk.

I'm still weirdly exhausted and wired after the run-in with the orc, but my body perks up in a different way at being this close to him. My heart beats a little faster, and a live wire runs from his touch right down to the soft core between my legs. Wowsers. Apparently, danger does it for me. I try not to lean into him and fail.

"If you don't feel comfortable, I could just put you in a cab and send you home," he suggests. He sounds a little husky, and I try not to read too much into it. But his body feels surprisingly soft as he wraps an arm around my waist, letting me lean into him.

"No, I... let's go," I say, feeling a blush rise to my cheeks, and darting my eyes from his.

I'm still catching my breath when we walk, wrapped around each other like it's the end and not the beginning of our night together.

Chapter Six

TOM

I resist the urge to bury my head into Summer's hair as we walk back to my house. It's more of an apartment, really, built into a converted warehouse. I usually don't like people seeing where I live. Right now I don't mind at all.

I could smell her from the first second I saw her in the office - long dark hair falling in unruly waves around her naked shoulders. She was a vision, and dangerous for my control.

I rely on the veneer of business - the careful restraint, the layers of perfume and suits - to keep my savagery in check. She's showing far too much skin tonight for me to feel civilized. And her scent makes me think of hunting, smelling the fear of prey.

Maybe Olivia is right, and she's one of the legendary mystics - a throwback from a time when our people traveled more freely into this realm. If she is, she's the first one I've ever met.

I look down at her, tucked beneath my arm. She looks incredible. Her dress clearly outlines small but shapely breasts, and floats around lean and muscular thighs. It's simple and elegant - she's a sharp contrast to the Sydney socialites I tried dating when I first established my identity as an entrepreneur. It was then I learned human women can't be trusted unless they have something to gain from a partnership. Those women were a different kind of hunter to me, but I recognize my own.

Summer doesn't seem like a hunter. She wears almost no makeup or scent, and she looks innocent - ready to be ravaged. Her skin is so soft. But she has a stubborn will. It's not surprising the orc today wanted to pin her down. A surge of protectiveness and anger rises in me.

One of my kind attacked her, and there's no excuse for it. I'll send Olivia to hunt the orc down and reprimand him further - it will only take one orc attacking a human to set the humans against us.

Fortunately, Summer seemed too shaken up to notice the words of her attacker when he referred to my royalty. She still seems too shaken up to notice much at all. My orc senses are sharper than humans, even in this form, and I can hear her heart fluttering wildly.

She needs to be protected - to be safe. Any further shocks will be bad for her, and the last thing she'll want to see right now is another orc. But there was a plan for this evening, and even though it didn't start the way I expected, I can't turn my back on my duty.

So I steer us down Cathedral street. There are other routes to my house, but this street is a congregation point for the homeless, and these days they are mostly orcish refugees. There's a police station on the street, so it should feel safe, but sometimes it doesn't, and dark is quickly approaching.

The first of the huddled homeless comes into view. Summer stiffens beside me incrementally. "We aren't far, but this is the quickest way," I lie.

She stays silent as we pass a group of orcish men seated together, their big green shoulders hunched over to make them seem smaller. Their tusks are filed short. Still, they look like warriors. Some of them look up as we pass. They meet my eyes but do nothing to give away my role as their leader. They sniff the air and cast curious glances at Summer before bowing their heads again.

It's warm, but their clothing is more ragged than I would like. Olivia is here once a day to take care of them, but they will only take enough charity to avoid starving. We tried to control the alcohol when we first got here but found it useless. Not even my brother can control it. They need something to numb the pain of being unwanted and so far from home.

Summer's heart picks up a notch, but she stays glued to my side, which I enjoy for more than one reason. Now my people have seen us together, she's safe from any further attacks, regardless of whether she's a mystic.

We pass more groups of men, almost thirty altogether.

I glance down at her. Compassion pools in her eyes, but it's nothing more than a normal human reaction.

A pang of disappointment hits my chest, surprising me. I've never believed in the mystics, but Summer... she made me wonder. But if she was a mystic, she would surely have revealed herself as she walked through so many orcs.

When we're past the group, the street breaks out into a wide-open space near the water. It's a more developed area, the fading light revealing the wharf where I live and the restaurants lining it underneath.

We walk along the river, still in an embrace. My protectiveness and urge to demonstrate she belongs to me made me stay with my arm around her in the alleyway. But she doesn't move away, even with the intimidation of so many orcs gone.

Her heartbeat slows, and she sighs. I expect her to pull away, but she stays where she is. "It's so sad," she says, and the feeling in her words moves me.

"That's why I want to help," I say.

There's a pause as she processes this. "I believe you," she says, and again, I feel the weight in her words, as if she's changed her mind about me. "I've got a sense for people, and I could feel your compassion when we walked through that alleyway."

"A sense for people?" That captures my interest. The mystics were empaths and sometimes even predicted the future.

"Yes. It's silly, really. Irrational. I can tell things sometimes from simple interactions. It's probably just good observation skills." She brushes it off as if she's sorry she mentioned it.

There's nothing in her words that signifies the strength of the empathic connection to others mystics have. She's using a turn of phrase, like the humans do. Again, a part of me is disappointed. But she intrigues me. "I don't think it's irrational to have instincts. It's a gift, and it shows you care enough to notice things."

She's quiet at that, as if I've given her cause to pause. It's strange to me that she would dismiss her instincts so quickly. Orcs value our instincts, but many humans listen to theirs also. It makes me wonder what causes her to doubt her own.

"I do wonder, with your resources... you could end their homelessness easily, yes?"

Frustration wells in me and I guard my words carefully. I wish to be honest with her, but can't tell her the whole truth. "I wish it were that easy," I say. "The orcs are a proud people. They will accept work, but not charity. If they felt I was hiring them for charity, they would turn it down"

There's much more I could say. Instead I say, "I think there's a better solution."

"Is that why he called you my lord? That orc? Because you've offered to hire him before?"

"Yes," I lie.

We walk in silence for a beat. In the silence, I worry she'll ask more thorny questions. I ask, "Your empathy - is that why you reacted when I was angry at the professor?" I was unreasonable, I know it. I was reacting to something I didn't want to hear.

"I'm sorry about the water," she says.

"I'm sorry I wasn't ready to hear his idea," I say, meaning it.

I'm surprised by myself. It's not common I admit fault. I find myself dawdling, not ready for the conversation to end. It's not just the heat either - there's something about

Summer, as if there's a hidden layer of her - a confident woman waiting to come out, cloaked in uncertainty. "Did you want to work with the orcs to help people?" I ask.

She hesitates before responding and I wonder if I've said the wrong thing. But then she says, "I picked my job because I wanted to help the most people. That was the idea anyway. But it feels like helping people is very far away from what I do day to day."

"Maybe that's okay. Most of my day isn't spent helping anyone, but ultimately, I want my money to do good in the world."

"Is that why you want to help the orcs?" she asks.

"Yes, that's it," I cover. I skirt the reality of my life - hustling in whatever way I can make money best, in the hope money might be the key to saving my people. It's incredibly frustrating to sit in meetings all day with humans, but this is the sacrifice of leadership. I rarely take anything for myself.

I glance down at Summer. She might not be a mystic, but I'm not sorry to be bringing her up to my apartment. I haven't felt this relaxed in months - maybe years.

Thoughts of her spread out on my bed in that dress are intrusive, unwanted, and ridiculous. I've tried sex in this form. It's pleasant enough, but it feels like my senses are muted. Besides, most human women do little for me.

Summer, however, is different. It's my turn for my heart to beat faster as we get closer to my apartment. Only across a street now, and we're at the entrance.

The weather breaks as we step across the road. The heat gives way to a rush of sudden downpour, forcing us to break contact and find shelter in the corner of a nearby building. It's only because of that we see the reporter.

Summer spots him before I do. I'm distracted by watching the rain run in rivulets down her naked shoulders, soaking her dark curls into her skin, when she turns to me.

"That man outside the restaurant under the wharf... he looks shifty, don't you think?" she asks, loudly enough to be heard over the rain.

I look up and instantly recognize the man. He's a slimy reporter who's been trying to get an interview with me for weeks. His look is generic, but he broke his hand a week ago and I can see the cast from here.

Summer's right - he looks shifty, like he's waiting for me. "It is. Steve Little. A scumbag from the East paper. Looks like he's trying to ambush me," I say. "It's okay, there's a back door. He won't see us."

We're close to the back entrance, and I take her down a side street, using a key to enter a service building. A quick lift ride down and then a short corridor walk to the apartment block, and up in another lift.

The lift rides are full of her scent, and the rooms feels too small. My senses feel heavier than usual, every sense tuned in to her movements, the feel of her in the room.

She hasn't touched me again since the rain broke, so I don't reach for her. I was comforting her, after all. And then marking her as mine with my people. I have no right to her apart from that. I'm also conscious of how much I want contact back. Is that healthy? I'm not used to distractions. My people mean everything to me. Olivia's right - I'm all work, no play. I thought that's how it had to be. Summer makes me wonder.

I run my hand through my hair and look anywhere else but at her.

The second lift is glass. The big empty wharf warehouse stretches around us. Apartment doors line every floor, and there are railings around the walkways that line the big empty space. Outside, there's an ongoing downpour.

Maybe sex will get her out of my system.

The thought is as intrusive as images of her naked, and the maddening urge to brush back her hair or run my tongue along the soft skin on her neck.

Sex wasn't my intention when I invited her back to my house - she had looked pale and shaken. And she was emanating so much scent I was worried that unescorted, the next orc she saw would attack her. I suppress the shame at the fact I was the one who'd invited her into the area where the orc population lived.

The rain hammers down hard on the tin roof of the old wharf shed, drowning out any chance of conversation as the lift arrives on my floor.

The doors open, and I take a big gulp of fresh air. The fresh air brings clarity - sex is a bad idea.

I stomp out of the lift and ahead of her, leading her to my apartment door, thoughts whirling.

I've done my duty - I've tested whether she's a mystic, and she's not. That means sex would be nothing but entertainment, nothing but a distraction.

And besides, I'm drunk on this woman. I've had sex with human women before, but it requires a restraint I'm not sure I'll be able to keep with Summer. I can't ensure my orc won't come out with her.

By the time I get to my front door, I'm firm in my determination - I'll make sure she's alright and send her straight back home. I unlock the front door almost angrily, not caring what she must be thinking of me, and push open the door, holding my breath as she walks past me into my apartment.

Chapter Seven

SUMMER

The doors to the warehouse are all bright colors, pops of chic against the industrial gray. I follow him and notice him carefully navigating around me without touching.

I missed his touch after I pulled away from him in the sudden downpour outside. His touch surprised me - how closely he held me, as if he cherished the contact, or hadn't been held in a long time.

But now I notice the tension at the corners of his mouth again and the set of his shoulders tightening. Perhaps I stayed too long in his embrace and overstayed my welcome. He's a billionaire, after all.

I have to remind myself that a few hours ago, I thought he was a total ass. But tonight, he seemed to relax - almost melt into my touch. For a while there I forgot he was Tom

Johnson. This warehouse is a reminder - it's incredibly quiet inside, despite the cavernous space.

Tom stops at a bright blue door close to the lift on the second to top floor. I step in close behind him and notice his shoulders tense. I keep my distance as he unlocks the door and ushers me in ahead of him.

Inside, it's hard not to gasp. It's beautiful. His apartment stretches upwards across two floors, and the wall across from the door is entirely made of glass panels. They stretch up high, with the top floor set out like a loft. The bottom floor features an open plan with a dining table, a kitchen and a lounge. The kitchen is modern and steel. In the lounge are comfortable-looking black couches with matching throws neatly folded over them. All the seats look slightly oversized, emanating luxury, and the room is finished with polished wood, black trims and rough brick.

Outside, the storm is a gray mist washing over the view of the harbor and the ships outside.

I've seen the interior of these wharf apartments before - online, many times. And I've seen a dozen interviews with Tom. No journalist has ever seen inside this apartment. This is a custom job, built to a billionaire's specifications, and apart from the warehouse chic, it looks nothing like the lobby outside. It also looks - comfortable.

Despite the beauty and lavishness, it feels like a personal sense of style is marked on it - it feels like a retreat. It makes me feel conscious that I'm intruding under false pretenses.

Anxiety crawls in my stomach suddenly. If I needed a reminder that this man is a billionaire, this is it.

Despite holding on to him for far longer than was decent tonight, I still don't know him. I believed him when he said he meant the best for the orcs. I could hear it in his voice. But now I wonder about his intentions, bringing me into what is clearly his private space.

How far would I go for a story? I lick my lips at the thought of what might happen here.

"Amazing view," I say, letting it distract me from my nerves. And follow him as he walks me over to the glass wall. He keeps at least a meter between us.

"I like it," he says, simply, but I can hear the pride in his voice.

Down below, men run around on the deck of one of the naval ships in port. It's still a working harbor, despite the luxury apartment block built on it. From here, I can see the secret entrance we took across the road. And Steven, standing nearby. He's clearly given up his vigil at the base of the building, but why is he near the secret entrance? Tom follows my line of sight and frowns.

"That can't be good," I say aloud.

"No," he says. "But at least we can see where he is from here. I'll get my people on it. In the meantime, we should eat here. Are you feeling better after your attack?"

I'm not surprised by the question, but the tone behind it. He's all business. There goes the idea that this was a seduction - he must have genuinely been concerned for my safety. I'm disappointed that I won't get to see more of his inner life. I assume that's the reason for the sinking feeling in my stomach, anyway.

Perhaps this is what all the women he's brought here feel like. Maybe I should count myself lucky that his distant tone happened before we had sex. This could be his bachelor pad and the reason he hasn't shown it in public is to impress women like me. Maybe he's had it designed to give this combination of intimacy and personal touch. But I don't think so. And if that were the case, why isn't he pleased to have me here?

He seems edgy too - fidgety, like he can't wait for me to leave.

"You should be able to smell a story," my editor says. Is that what's going on here now? Is that why I'm sorry I'm not staying?

"You can use the guest bathroom if you need to dry off while I take care of this," Tom suggests, polite but distant.

Gone is the man who had his arms around me only a few minutes ago. My head is still spinning at the change.

He leads me upstairs. There are three doors, and we pass two. He stops at the end door and opens it while already reaching for his phone. I should be happy he's not being sleazy or predatory, but instead I feel irrationally dismissed by the billionaire. He's texting someone already as the door swings open.

Of course, what that means is he's not looking when I see the paintings.

On every wall, there are traditional paintings of orcs engaged in carnal acts with humans. Specifically, male orcs with enormous bodies and erect penises. They tower over female humans as they perform various sexual acts. The women are in various state of undress, but in every painting, there are the diaphanous and transparent white shifts of a mystic.

"Um..." I choke.

He looks up from his phone, and his eyes widen. His nostrils flare, and for a second, I swear his eyes go red. Then it calms as quickly as it came on, and the tightly controlled Tom is back. "My bodyguard... she stays here sometimes, and these are her rooms. These are traditional orcish..."

"Heiros Gamos," I finish, stepping into the room further. I can't look at him right now - he's so obviously uncomfortable. That leaves me looking at the paintings, which are fortunately quite riveting. They're famous, but I've only ever seen them online. "Of course I know what they are - they're the only artwork we have from the orcs home world. Depicting ritual offerings by mystics in exchange for orcish protection. Replicated by human artists working with orcs. This is quite a collection."

"Clearly she wanted something to remind her of home," he says stiffly.

"I can see that." I'm finding it hard not to smile at his discomfort.

"You seem to be recovered from your distress. I'll let you get dried off and take care of the reporter, and then I'll call you a cab home," he says stiffly, and closes the door behind him.

With him gone, I look further around the room. It's gorgeous, in the same industrial chic as downstairs, and just as cozy. The queen-sized bed has a dark wood carved ornate base with two tall, curving posts at the head, like horns, and it's made up with crisp white sheets. It doesn't look slept in recently.

Could it be that this explains why Tom's so interested in the orc community? I think of Olivia - she's a strong, tall orc warrior, with impressive musculature and a cheeky grin. If they're lovers, Olivia seems like the kind of person who'd want to shout it to the world. But then why did she get my number for Tom? There's definitely some kind of story here.

I walk from painting to painting, taking pictures. A lascivious scene keeps drawing me back - an orc has a woman suspended by one leg, and his enormous tongue is pressed against her sex. I stifle a laugh at Tom's obvious discomfort at me seeing these images. Even if he kicks me out now, I already have my story.

I ignore the dull clench of shame in the pit of my stomach about violating Tom's trust. He's hot and cold and incredibly strange, but if he's in love with an orc, that explains a lot. And I like Olivia. But this is the gossipy story my editor will love.

I step into the bathroom, as spacious and luxurious as I would expect, and find a hair dryer and a towel. I use the towel, and when I'm done, I have a message waiting for me from Emily and slump onto the perfectly made bed to check it.

> *How's the date with the billionaire? - Emily*

> *I'm at his apartment - Summer*

OH MY GOD - Emily

But it doesn't look like I'm his type - Summer

Gay??? - Emily

I think of the sparks that hit when I touched Tom Johnson. I send Emily one of the photos from the wall, knowing I can trust my sister won't send it on any further.

!!! You got your story! Also, gross - Emily

My eyes drift to the nearest painting. The woman in the image is on her knees, tongue licking the end of a huge penis. Something low in my belly stirs in excitement.

There's definitely some disappointment at knowing Tom isn't interested, but the last time I was involved with a man, he betrayed me.

Oh, I don't know, they have something :P - Summer

I take some time uploading the photos I took to the cloud and deleting them from my phone. Then I go into the bathroom, turn the hairdryer back on, and sneak out of the room. The fact Tom didn't expect me to see the orc photos means there could be all kinds of interesting things to find in this place.

Chapter Eight

TOM

"She's in your apartment?" Olivia laughs down the phone.

"Yes, and I showed her the guest room," I say icily. My face is still burning, but I'm not angry at Olivia. I'm angry at myself for not checking what she'd done to the room before showing Summer in.

Olivia laughs harder. "Wait, is she staying the night?"

I look out the window. The reporter is now standing with three other people, deep in conversation. "That wasn't the plan, but with these reporters roving around, I'm not comfortable escorting her out."

"What was the plan then, dear brother? Why did you bring her to your tower of solitude in the first place? First human you've invited in there, isn't she?"

"You wanted us to go on this date, remember?"

"To check if she was a mystic, yes. And you've already established she isn't, along with claiming her to the entire orc community. Which shouldn't be an issue unless she suddenly develops an exotic taste in men. You know she isn't a mystic, and you still invited her back," she points out. "You could have put her in a cab at any point until now, and you've resisted many other damsels in distress in the past."

I have no response to that, so I change the subject. "Find out what's going on with the reporters and get more security on the building."

"Already done. Just sent you a message," she says.

I flick to messenger and open the image she sent me. I swear out loud. It's a picture of the orc pinning Summer against the wall, and me intervening. Summer's face is clearly visible. She'll need a disguise to get out of here tonight. I put the phone back to my ear.

"Er, you still looking out your window, bro?" Olivia asks.

I scan the street. "Yes, why?" It's then I see it - protestors joining the three journalists, holding placards, undeterred by the rain, heading towards my building. More of them than last week - a lot more.

"They've advertised a huge sit-in outside your building. It's all over social media. I'd advise you to stay with your house guest for a while longer."

"How long?" I don't mean to growl, but having Summer here unsettles me. I was ready to throw her straight into a cab after her seeing the paintings in Olivia's guest room.

"Honestly? All night."

"Are you playing with me, Olivia? We know she's not a mystic."

"I'm sorry bro, but that protestor we saw yesterday isn't harmless. She's mingled with some serious characters and has connections to organized crime."

My head suddenly hurts - a flash headache. "This is about the shooting isn't it?" Local drug dealers have had an issue with the orcs after that incident with the shooting. It's caused nothing but a headache. They don't like anyone being tougher than them, and Olivia has been running interference to keep the gangs away from the orcs.

"Yup. Honestly, it's pure luck that one of the gangs hasn't got an orc on their team yet."

I snort. This is why I had such a bad reaction to the professor's idea. The orc the professor had wanted to be a hero spent most of his time passed out on various substances. He was a good friend of my brother Evan. We had him locked up in a warehouse for his own safety but could only control him sedated, and Evan insisted we let him out. I wish I could trust my brother could keep him safe.

Olivia goes on. "You're raising the profile of orcs, and raising sympathy for them, and I'm worried they're going to go after you, using a protest as an excuse. As your head of security, I recommend complete lockdown. No leaving your apartment for 24 hours. I'm worried about your safety. Can you handle that with the houseguest?"

"I haven't even eaten dinner yet," I say, exasperated.

"I'll send a guy over with something for you," she says. "You'd better let your friend know she can't leave either. You're in lockdown now until I say so. And if you can check your friend's handbag for a gun, do so."

"She doesn't have a Gr'aking gun," I say violently. "I'm pretty sure she only had a phone on her."

"Well, she might have had one tucked into her underwear. I'll feel better if you check for me anyway, and I'll do a background check on her here in the meantime," she says, and hangs up.

Summer is coming down the stairs. Her hair is dry but her dress is still damp, clearly outlining her soft breasts. There's no way that dress could cover a gun without me noticing. My mouth waters and I look away, swallowing. So not the time.

"There's a protest starting outside," I say. "My security has asked for us to stay put for now. I'm sorry about this, we can't go anywhere until morning. You can stay in the guest room. Dinner is arriving soon."

I know I'm looking anywhere but her. The rain is still loudly hammering onto the glass outside.

She looks relatively calm, but I can hear her pulse quicken alarmingly. I resist the urge to step forward to comfort her. I'm not sure if I'll be able to step away again.

I'm being absurd. I know nothing about her except that she smells good, she didn't like me being rude to her colleague, and she agreed to a date. She may have leaned into my touch after her shock tonight, but she's kept her distance since, and I'm not sure if she trusts me.

"I've been told it's all over social media," I say, to reassure her I'm not making this entire thing up. "If you need to contact anyone to let them know where you are, that should explain it."

"No, I... there's nobody I need to call," she says. "I'm new to the city."

"Ah."

"My parents check in on me by phone, though." She sounds slightly worried.

"There's a universal charger in the bedroom," I assure her. "And also... You don't have to worry. I recognize this isn't the evening we had planned. I won't make any advance on you to take advantage of the situation."

She looks me full in the face as if startled. Her eyes are soft, and brown, and again I'm strangely reminded of my homeland. I find myself speaking again. "Among my... family... we consider it a great dishonor to put guests in danger. And I believe I've done so tonight."

She protests, and I raise a hand to stop her.

"Please... They took pictures of us together with the orc. If you leave here tonight the press will know, and I can't promise you won't be harassed after this. The best we can hope for is that they don't find out who you are."

She nods, acquiescing. Her face is pale now, and I'm glad she fully understands the impact of the press's attentions. Again, the urge to reach out, to touch her shoulder, almost makes me move. Instead, I step back.

"While dinner arrives, you are welcome to take a shower and get more comfortable. I believe Olivia leaves some spare sweats here. And I have some things to take care of in my study." Then I turn and retreat upstairs, to my study, two doors down from the room she's sleeping in.

When the door shuts, I lean against it and breathe deeply. Her scent is less prominent here and I can clear my head. I hope she puts on Olivia's sloppy evening clothing so I can stop picturing her in that damned dress. I force myself to sit at my computer and scroll through emails.

It's only fifteen minutes later the doorbell rings. I haven't gotten a damn thing done.

I hear the shower running from the guest room as I leave my study. When I open the front door one of my human drivers hands me a bag of delicious smelling Thai food. I know what the order is without checking - a chicken Pad Thai and green beef curry with rice. Olivia knows what I like.

I pause with the bag on the kitchen counter. The shower is still running but won't be for much longer.

Before I stop to think, I head up the stairs.

I could resist before, when she was about to be bundled into a cab and leave, but now with her staying the night... I want her and I can no longer deny it.

I open the guest room door, taking a risk that she will have shut the bathroom door. She has, and her dress is laid out on the bed along with some sweats. Her shoes are kicked into a corner, her phone charging by the bed.

Knowing she's naked behind that door drives me to distraction, but I stay focused.

I won't ignore Olivia's warnings. There's movement against the orc community and suddenly this captivating girl comes out of nowhere. I might want her, but I have a people to keep safe.

I click on her phone and check the screen. A message from someone called Emily - 'You got this' - and a picture of Summer with an older couple that look like her parents standing outside a hardware store.

"What are you doing?" she asks. I turn. She's standing staring at me, hair still wet. The shower is running behind her. She's caught me looking at her phone, with the screen lit up like I just pressed a button.

My heart races, but I learned diplomacy in the royal court and then the boardroom. I can lie through my teeth. "I knocked, but you couldn't hear me over the shower. A message came through for you. Food is ready. I'll give you a few minutes," I say, and walk out.

I suppress my shame. I can't regret getting caught snooping. Summer is in my home, and there are secrets here nobody knows except my people. It might make her distrust me, but I'm not alone in the world, and my responsibilities come before my needs. I go straight into my study and call Olivia. "What do you have on her?" I ask abruptly.

"I thought you didn't think she was a threat?" Olivia teases. I ignore her until she goes on, voice changing into sharp professionalism. "She doesn't have a gun, and I couldn't find anything. The intern agency looks legit. She's young, apparently fresh to Sydney from a small town in South Australia, with no real working experience. But I can't find any flight details in her name, just the intern agency notes. So it could be a good cover story, Tom."

"So you found nothing," I say.

"I found nothing conclusively bad, but nothing conclusively good, either. Don't let her have access to any secrets and you should still be able to have yourself a delightful party tonight."

My orc is restless and not being able to transform tonight is challenging enough, so the growl I let down the phone is louder than it would be if anyone else was around. "That's not exercising caution," I say.

"Man, she has gotten to you, hasn't she?" Olivia says. "I mean it though - you need to blow off some steam, and there's no reason not to have some fun if she doesn't know anything."

I hang up without ceremony.

Olivia's always been better at compartmentalizing than me. If Summer is hiding something, she could be involved with the protestors, so I can't let her get closer to me. Olivia has it right that Summer's under my skin, her scent lingering even now in my nostrils.

Sex with women in this form in the past has always meant a level of control, even in the throes of passion. The way I've dealt with it is to remain dispassionate, which ruins the sense of pleasure even before I begin. I already know I can't keep my control with Summer, and that makes me dangerous for her, and vice versa.

No, I can't just have my fun with her. Not until Olivia finds out more. For tonight, Summer is my guest and nothing more.

CHAPTER NINE

SUMMER

I wake up in a strange bed, face down, starving. My stomach grumbles - I only picked at the Thai food last night.

My pulse races. It takes a few seconds to register I'm in Tom Johnson's house. I slow my breathing intentionally. It takes longer than it should, but I don't have my pills with me tonight. I'm sure I can manage until morning.

I throw a hand out, grabbing for my phone. It's 5am. Social media says the protest downstairs has turned into a vigil now the rain has gone. It seems as if the protestors are incredibly determined - suspiciously so. This is turning out to be a bigger story than I planned.

My editor was right - I followed the story and was being rewarded.

The last message I received from her was only a few moments after Tom had left the room. She had sent a blurry photo of Tom and the orc from outside the restaurant, me looking wide-eyed in the background.

I look shaken up, but fortunately I can't see the rage that surged through me reflected in the photo. I was too shocked at Tom's intervention at that point, I think.

I was sure they'd fire me, but she followed up with another quick text.

Good work. Keep it up - Editor Sandra

She'd carefully kept the message vague, because she's a professional. Meanwhile I'd forgotten to change her name in my phone before going undercover. Rookie mistake.

If Tom had been only a few minutes later, he would have seen I had an editor saved in my phone. What would he have done then? Throw me out into the street and the protestors? Maybe that was better than the sinking pit of guilt in my stomach at having almost been caught.

Somehow, lying to Tom is making me feel worse than the prospect of losing this story. There's something earnest about him, under the hostility of the billionaire. He really does care about the orcs. Probably because of his girlfriend.

And all the sneaking around upstairs didn't get me anywhere - my trick with leaving the hairdryer on earlier didn't help. The doors upstairs were locked. Who locks doors in their own house?

It was in that state that I'd gone down to dinner, and I'd barely been able to eat a thing. Tom was quiet too, distant and as stiff as he'd been since we got to his apartment. It was a relief when he retired to his study, claiming work to do.

I'd gone back to my room and scrolled through the news feeds, finding out as much as I could about the protest outside. It was suspicious they were so determined. This wasn't just xenophobia. There were rumors of a link to organized crime after that orc had intervened to stop the shooting a few weeks ago. The same incident the professor had mentioned.

I read more. The heroic deed was accidental - he'd been walking past, and his tough skin had stopped the bullets. In a drunken rage, he'd attacked the shooter, knocking him unconscious, and walked away, leaving the shooter to be safely arrested by the police. Because he was drunk, surly and had left the scene, he wasn't quite the hero the professor was hoping he could be, but it had stirred up the organized crime in the city.

Could this protest be linked? It's likely Tom's bodyguard thinks it is.

None of these thoughts stop my stomach rumbling. And grabbing a snack is a perfect excuse to go exploring Tom's humble abode. Maybe some of the doors are unlocked now.

I leave my light off and push the door open, grateful for no creaks. The house is silent, and the door to the study next to my room is hanging open. I consider going directly in, but my stomach grumbles again. It'll make a better cover if I've got food in hand. So I tiptoe past the third room I assume is Tom's, and head downstairs. There's enough light coming in through the windows outside that I make the stairs easily.

The kitchen is as spacious as everything else in the place, with plenty of counter space. Everything looks new and untouched, which makes me think Tom Johnson doesn't cook much.

The fridge is easy enough to find and navigate. It's mostly empty apart from the takeaway, confirming my impressions Tom doesn't eat at home much. I find a bowl and a fork easily enough. I eat some Pad Thai cold, my stomach not caring and not wanting to risk the noise of a microwave.

I decide my cover is better with bowl in hand, so I willingly risk looking like an uncouth houseguest and take it up the stairs with me.

At the top of the landing, I pause. There are sounds coming from Tom's room, although there's no light on under the door.

What he does with his own time is none of my business, but if he's awake, I can't investigate his study safely.

I'm standing there wondering if I can risk it when I hear a loud thump. Then a crash.

"Tom?" I call out. I step closer to his door, listening hard. A loud snuffling and a muffled growl - a growl? Then a tinkle and a muffled curse.

"Tom?" Silence.

I should just move on past and ignore it. But the sounds don't sound normal. My editor's words ring in my head - follow the story. I put my half-finished bowl and fork down on the floor, to the side, out of the way.

"Tom, I'm coming in," I announce, but don't wait as I turn the handle and push open the door.

A giant orc is standing next to Tom's bed, naked, next to a smashed beside lamp. He's enormous - towering over the bed - with sharp tusks that curl from the sides of his jaw and an inhumanly, very erect, cock.

I scream.

He lunges at me, pushes me against the wall, and places a hand over my mouth with one hand, the other against my shoulder. I'm pinned in place, as much by his strength as by fear.

He grunts, and I stare up at his huge, dark green body. Proportioned like a man, he's much larger, at 7 feet tall, with a width and shoulders any bodybuilder would envy. He's bigger than the orc outside the restaurant - much bigger. Despite shoving me against the wall, he hasn't hurt me, but my body quivers.

There's a drumming in my blood, an excitement that's close to fear but not quite. It's like when I have an episode - the thing my parents worry about the most. This is how I felt when I attacked Steve, but much, much stronger.

If I wasn't being pinned down, I know with certainty I would be attacking him. And that wouldn't be a good idea.

I know orcs as warriors and conquerors - they would rape and pillage when they conquered, in the old stories. But they're just stories, right? Now they're civilized - trying to fit into society. Like this orc here, breaking into Tom Johnson's home. Or the orc who attacked me today. My thoughts swirl. I try to stop thinking.

The orc leans in, and his tusks cage around my neck. Irrationally, I think that if he was any closer, I could bite him. He sniffs my hair, inhaling deeply. He licks an enormous tongue over his lips and emits a low, primal growl. A zing thrills through my core at the sound.

I hold my breath, not sure what happens next. Will he eat me? Rape me? Instead, he lets me down gently and steps back.

I breathe in for a second, heart racing, gaze roaming up his body, averting my eyes from his erection. He grunts again, and I look up at his face, and into the familiar hawk-like sharpness of his eyes.

"Get out," he says. "And forget what you saw here."

His voice is familiar too. "Tom?" I ask, the realization too shocking to process.

"I said get out!" he shouts, and emphasizes with a growl as he pushes me out the door, slamming it shut behind me.

CHAPTER TEN

TOM

The door slams shut, but it doesn't stop her damned scent. I didn't mean to turn tonight - was expecting not to, but I fell asleep and in my dreams, I was chasing her. When I woke up, I had turned. I haven't done that since I was a pup.

My nostrils are still flared with the scent of her. And my cock is rock hard. I shouldn't be surprised. My apartment is saturated with her scent, and the spell that shifts me into a man takes some control to keep in place.

Right now, it's taking all my control not to break through into her room and ravage her, or at least lick her from head to toe to see if she tastes as good as she smells.

I shake my head. I sit awkwardly back on the floor beside the smashed bedside lamp, legs crossed, trying to meditate to put the spell back in place.

Thoughts intrude on my calm. My gut churns. How could I be so foolish? Summer tests my control. I invited a human into my home, and now she's seen my true state. I've jeopardized everything I want for my people.

She has distracted me from the start. My instincts have been pure orc, as much as I've tried to fight it. My civilized veneer is just that.

That beautiful scent of hers is soiled now by the acrid smell of her fear and thickened by an underlying waft of arousal. It's confusing, but human women's sexuality is complicated, as Olivia keeps telling me. And even with that bitter scent of fear, I have to fight my erection down.

There's nothing for it. I'll have to talk to her. But first I must get my orc under control.

It takes a full fifteen minutes.

I try to clear my mind, but it's full of Summer. I've left her alone in my house, and she now knows what I am. She could be hiding anything. I didn't get a full report on her - I don't know if she is who she says she is. She could be organized crime, or worse - government. The anxiety of it eventually makes my erection go down, and I get my breathing under control enough for my shape to return to a man's. I change into different sweats - the ones I was wearing were shredded in the change. And I take a deep breath before leaving my room to see whether Summer's still in the apartment.

I find her sitting at the smoked glass dining table with a bowl of cold Pad Thai. She's not eating it, she's sitting and staring into space, until she notices me and her eyes zone in on mine.

I keep my expression closed, as much of the businessman as I can muster. I wish I were wearing a suit.

"May I sit?" my voice drips with icicles. She nods. Her heartbeat is going a mile a minute, but she says nothing. Perhaps she isn't sure what to say, which is understandable. Perhaps she's waiting for me to break out into an orc again.

I must be careful, or she will run, and although I have a guard outside the door, he won't know to keep her in. And it shouldn't come to that. This is a negotiation. I'm good at those.

"You understand you can tell nobody about this," I begin. "My family was gifted years ago with the ability to turn into humans. When we came here, I was uniquely placed to trade on behalf of my people. It would be problematic if my true nature came out."

She nods.

"In your world, orcs are considered brutish, and stupid." She winces at my honesty. "It would jeopardize my standing in the community if my true nature were to come out. In return for your silence, I can offer you a funded role with the professor, to continue your work with the orc cause. Or if you'd prefer, you can name your price and we can part ways. I trust you."

She stiffens, as I thought she would, but her heartbeat hasn't slowed. There's something honorable about her, and I thought she would bristle at the mention of a bribe, but she still says nothing. I wait.

"May I... see it? The transformation?" She sounds curious and excited. "It might... help me figure out what to do next."

I don't need heightened senses to smell the lie. There's no way seeing me transform will help her decide. I expected fear, or shock. Curiosity is something I didn't expect.

My orc scratches at me from the inside, wanting to be out around this woman. I push down the leap of unreasonable hope in my chest, and the orc down with it, and consider.

She looks away from me, but I can see anticipation in every line of her body.

I should say no. But the damage is done, and perhaps I'm as curious as she is. "You may see the transformation again. And then we'll continue our discussion."

I put my hand on the table and let the transformation happen slowly. A green color creeps onto my skin as my hand expands. The color creeps up my arm, heading towards my face.

That's all I mean to show her - to help prove that she saw what she did. But her face, staring at my hand, is captivated, and she leans forward and ever so gently strokes my claw.

My skin tingles at her touch, and in a rush, the rest of my orc bursts free. I huff in surprise and irritation. Another pair of sweats ruined. I growl at her before I can control myself.

To my shock, she slaps me full in the face, her face contorted in rage. My orc reacts, a hand around her throat and lifting her up out of her chair before I can stop myself, but she kicks me hard in the shin and I drop her quickly.

Then she hisses at me and lunges forward to kiss me full on the lips.

She's a wild thing, claws digging in and legs hiked up around me as she bites and licks at my lips.

I'm still catching my breath when she pulls away suddenly, looking horrified.

"I... I'm so sorry..." she says. "I... get these episodes." Her hands are to her mouth, and she flees up the stairs to her room, leaving me panting and wondering what the hell just happened.

Chapter Eleven

SUMMER

I slam the door to the guest room, as if that will do anything useful. Tom can get in any time he likes - it's his house. And I've just thrown myself on him like a lunatic. I press myself back against the door and take a moment to recover.

It's difficult - my pulse is racing, my breathing shallow. I've soaked my underwear with my own juices. Orc senses are heightened, or so I've been led to believe - could he have smelled me?

Before I have time to be embarrassed about that, the sight of his huge, hard orcish body comes back to me, and my nipples pebble. He's attractive as a human, but as an orc... That billionaire veneer - the coiffed hair and polished style - is stripped away. He's raw and untamed, and when he growled, something in me snapped.

He even smells wild - like the bush after the rain - with something deeper tangled in it, something spiced and more dangerous. It makes me think of jungles I've never been to - places where the orcs were native, running free and savage in their own lands.

I flick the light on and the images on the wall stare at me - the one where the orc is licking between the woman's legs is particularly captivating right now. Pinned, wearing nothing but a transparent slip, nipples grazing the delicate fabric.

My blood rushes in my ears, and I have the sudden urge to fling open the door and attack Tom again, to see whether he can ease the urgent pressure inside me.

In desperation, I slip a hand into my underwear, and in seconds, a wave of pleasure floods me. My first orgasm in months - over an orc. Over Tom Johnson, the orc.

I shake my head. It makes sense now that the bodyguard is his mate. My heart is pinched, but my body is recovering from its insanity. I entered Tom's room without invitation. He didn't approach me. He didn't reach for me in his house - in fact, he's been avoiding me. I don't know what his relationship is with his bodyguard, but I don't want to be caught in the middle of some crazy orc jealous game.

But the fact is - Tom Johnson, tech billionaire, is secretly an orc. I have my story. My stomach turns at the idea of betraying him, but I steel myself. Nobody said leaving home was going to be easy. After Steve stole my first story, I almost went home. It was Emily who convinced me that my instincts were excellent, and I knew there was something in Tom and his orc affinity. I never could have believed it was this big, though.

My eyes drift to the painting of the sacrifice licking the end of the orc's penis. Speaking of big... I'd never heard of orc and human sex working in real life, although according to the internet, many had tried.

I still have questions - why did Olivia set up our date? Why wouldn't Tom consider coming out to the public as the orc hero the professor proposed? And what is it about him that makes him able to turn? He said he was now doing business for his people - was he amassing a fortune for a reason? Is there a bigger plan for the orcs?

Now that my body is under control, the journalist in me rises to the surface. I need to follow the story - and I won't get answers in this room, alone.

I rip open the bedroom door, and run right into Tom as a man, his hand raised to knock on my door.

"We need to talk," he says, and turns and walks away from me, not waiting for me to follow.

A surge of anger wells up in me. I imagine jumping on his back, wrapping my hands around his neck, and... the images in my head shock me enough that my cheeks heat. Pushing down my rage, I take a deep breath and follow.

Tom sits across from me at the kitchen table. A crystal decanter of scotch sits between us, two glasses already poured. It's hard not to admire his composure - I can see he's tense, but he's holding it in. I access the professional in me, the journalist, and meet his upright posture and take a sip of scotch. My hand only shakes slightly.

A part of me - the part I find hard to control sometimes - wants me to slap the composure right out of him. Or kiss it out. I put the glass down with a clink.

"Are you a leader of your people?" My words are abrupt, needing to get out of my head. This is the best place to start.

"A king, yes."

I swallow. I wasn't expecting him to answer, but since he's sharing, I'm not stopping now. And apparently, neither is he.

He goes on. "That's why I funded the professor's research. It's clear our problems won't resolve themselves."

"Do you know how to get back to your world?"

"We do not. Nor would we want to."

"Are you involved with Olivia?" This wasn't the question I meant to ask next - not the most important one, but my words are bypassing my brain at this point.

"Olivia is my sister." *Sister.* I take another sip of scotch, needing it at this point. I keep the drink in my hand.

"Why did you ask me on a date with you?"

It's his turn to pause, as if looking for the right words. "Have you heard of the mystics?"

"The pictures in your..." I gesture upstairs vaguely, trying not to think too hard about the images on the walls.

"Yes. They have a human appearance, but they are in fact descendant from orcs. We had mystics in our homeland - only a few, and the ones we had were honored. But they existed there. The rumor is they exist in your land too, a throwback to a time when there was more travel between our realms."

"What does this have to do with me?" I ask, but inside I already know - he thinks I'm a mystic. That's why he risked bringing me here to his home. This is how desperate the orcs are for a solution to their plight. My conscience pangs.

"You have an..." he pauses, breathing deeply, and swallowing as if uncomfortable. "You have an unusually strong scent. To orcs, you smell good. I noticed it today, and it's likely why you were attacked outside the restaurant. It's also why I walked you past my people today, to mark you as mine. You won't be attacked like that again." He frowns at the memory of it. "And the orc who attacked you will be reprimanded."

"My *scent*? I'm sorry to disappoint you, but I'm not a mystic." I shake my head. "I'm just a girl from a small town."

"You may not know you have mystic blood in you. It only manifests around orcs. Although from old stories of the mystics, they have some orcish traits - blood lust and aggression. Do you have anything like that?"

I look at him sharply, wondering if he noticed my reaction to the orc today. His expression is eager - almost desperate. "I have an..." I hesitate. I would know if I were a mystic. But I feel compelled to share, anyway.

A flush rises to my cheeks and I fight the rising urge to snarl at him, to lash out. I close my eyes and take a deep breath. "I have an anxiety disorder. Being in Sydney makes it worse. I hadn't taken pills in years, but I'm back on medication for it. I had an... attack... a couple of weeks ago. So you see, I can't possibly be a mystic. I can barely function as a human being."

"How does the anxiety manifest?" he asks, eagerness lighting up his voice.

I shift in my chair but keep talking. It's a strange relief to talk about my disorder. Nobody else in Sydney knows about my condition except the doctor who renewed my pill prescription. "You know... anxiety. My heart races, I get hot and flustered, and in my case, I get angry. I can... lash out. It's dangerous. I can get myself into some bad situations. Like when the orc attacked me, my instinct was to hurt him back."

"And with me?" he asks, eyes glittering, and posture poised. "When I was an orc? Did you get the same sensations?"

I nod, too embarrassed to add the heightened level of arousal that went with it. It's hard to meet his eyes now, but he's still staring at me. "I couldn't possibly be a mystic. I'm so sorry to disappoint you," I say, shaking my head.

"Perhaps you are not," he says. "But you are the closest possibility my people have found in this world. And so, for the sake of an entire species in this world, would you be willing to try an experiment?"

"What does it involve?" I ask. My eyes flick to the images on the walls around us.

"There will have to be... an exchange of fluids," he says. "Not sex," he adds hastily. "There's no certainty you could handle an orc's size. But an oral exchange of sexual fluids from either party. It doesn't have to be direct contact, although it often is." His eyes become hazy at this last sentence, and he breathes in sharply. When he speaks next, his voice is tight, his speech rushed. "No pressure of course. If you are interested, join me in my chambers. Er, my room. If not, I shall forget the matter." Then he storms out, slamming the door after him.

I swallow. My body is on fire. Struggling to breath, I'm left dazed in his wake.

Chapter Twelve

TOM

I'm waiting in my bedroom, trying to control my breathing. My proposal is outrageous, and any human would turn it down. Unless Summer believes on some level she has orc blood, or she's compassionate enough about our cause to try. She did intern at the Orc Rights Association, after all.

A small part of me hopes she's genuinely interested as much as I am.

Do I genuinely think she's a mystic, or am I just hoping to satisfy my lusts? It's a consideration I can't deny, and I push it down. As when I walked Summer through my people, they come first, my moral qualms second.

My heart leaps when she gives a small knock on the door. I clear my throat and say, "enter".

I hold my breath as she steps over the threshold. Nothing changes in the world except my heart rate. Hers is consistently racing.

She doesn't look scared, but then I'm still in the cloak of a man, standing next to my bed, clothes on.

I turn away from her when I pull off my sweatshirt and ball it into a hamper in my wardrobe. My work shirts are neatly lined up inside my wardrobe, and I focus on them to distract myself. I move slowly so she can back out if she needs to, and I step out of my pants.

I smell uncertainty from her for the first time - fear. It's not unexpected, but I curse inwardly. Maybe I'm going about this all wrong.

This feels like a business transaction, and I feel far too human. If I don't transform now, she'll have run before we've even started. I rip my underwear off quickly and let my body transform.

It's like a ripple from my feet to my head, and I let the air around me stop wavering before I turn to face her. Her scent hits me again, stronger in this form, and her uncertainty is gone, replaced with pure arousal.

Her pupils are huge, her chest heaving. My cock twitches to attention when she smiles a feral smile at me and licks her lips, ripping her own sweatshirt off and stepping out of her pants.

"Summer." I growl, taking in her hard nipples, the visible damp between her thighs. Her heart is beating so loudly I'm concerned for her. She doesn't respond, and my concern grows. She sniffs the air in a feral fashion and growls.

I step forward slowly. She doesn't seem aware of what's going on, her intelligent eyes foggy with a hungry lust as it tracks my penis. That's not right - mystics went into trances, but they still kept some sense of reason. Summer's face is slack. Perhaps the ritual will bring her back to herself.

"Summer," She visibly shudders at her name on my lips and I fall into the sing-song tone of ritual. "In your role as mystic, will you kneel and give tribute?"

She grunts and kneels, crawling forward on all fours, eyes focused on my penis. Despite my lust, I'm hesitant. This feral creature is not the woman I invited into my home. Still, I watch her every move, hunger in my eyes. My breath hitches when she reaches me, and I emit a low growl.

Through the fog of lust, I remember aspects of the ritual. "Hands behind your back."

She looks up at me through coy lashes and smiles as she does as I ask. I tower over her, but I don't feel in control right now, even when she lowers her eyes submissively.

Her heady scent wraps around me, so strong I can barely breathe.

I lift her chin with a careful hand. "Look at me, Mystic."

The wild lust in her eyes nearly undoes me, and I wrap a hand through her hair and lower her to my cock.

Her small mouth can only fit around the end, but she laps out a tongue and licks a shining pearl of pre-cum cresting around the tip. A shudder runs through me, and her grin becomes triumphant as she continues to lick and suck the end of me.

Her movement becomes more frantic, and she bites - a pleasant sensation in this form, but a worrying sign of her control. Gr'ak the dark lord, I could keep going. I want to keep going. But how much of her is in there right now, and how much is she going to hate me later?

"Summer, that's enough," I say, pulling her hair back and away from me.

"I haven't finished my tribute," she says huskily, and takes me further into her mouth, releasing her hands and tugging on my balls.

I can barely stand at the sensation, groaning deeply. I start to semi-consciously pump into her throat. My control is completely gone at the sensations of her wet mouth sucking on me, and it doesn't take long before I roar and cum hotly into her mouth.

Dazed, I can barely stand when she jumps up at me, thighs straddling my waist, and her sodden pussy pressed against me.

I roar and throw her back onto the bed. She's clawing like a wild thing and I'm forced to straddle her legs to stop them kicking, one hand holding her arms pinned above her head.

She moans wantonly, writhing beneath me. It's enough to make me hard again, but I say her name again, hoping to snap her out of it. "Summer, calm down."

She hisses at me and snaps. "I gave tribute," she says. "Now your turn."

She's right. The ritual is always an exchange, and although the conscious Summer might hate me later, this wild creature won't rest until I have paid her.

Keeping one hand on her wrists and ignoring her kicking legs, I plunge two fingers inside her with retracted claws. She instantly responds, thrusting into my fingers instead of flailing to escape. She's deliciously wet and soft, and I groan even as I pump until she screams in release and fluids wash over my hand.

I release her hands and watch as she slowly blinks back to herself. I'm completely exhausted, and my cock is once again hard as a rock.

Her heartbeat slows for the first time, and she looks up at me in shock, covers her mouth with her hand, and scrambles out of the room, slamming the door behind her.

I'm still in my orc form, and my erection is still very present. I'm struggling to get it under control when I hear her run into her bedroom. I assume she needs some space. But her steps continue all the way downstairs and out the front door of the apartment.

Oh Gr'ak, the Dark Lord, I'm in trouble.

I did not brief my security to keep her inside, and I'm not sure if my human guards would respond to keeping a woman locked up in my apartment.

I call Olivia.

She's asleep "Ugh," she says. "What time is it?"

"6am. Did you find out anything about Summer?"

"Never mind that. Did you enjoy your enforced down time?"

"Yes I did, and I found out Summer's probably a mystic. And now she's run away."

"What?" Olivia suddenly sounds more awake.

"I tried the ritual. She responded as the mystics do - but she couldn't control it, and wasn't fully conscious."

"You did the thing with the tribute? And the..."

"Yes," I say.

Olivia laughs hysterically down her phone. "That is some kinky old-school role-playing brother. I didn't know you had it in you."

"It was the only way to tell," I say irritably. "And you were right. She probably is a mystic, but there's something wrong. It's like she's not aware of her mystic side. I need some time to get her on our side to see if she could help the entire species. But I wanted to check what you found out about her identity. I need to know where she is. If she has family, they could be mystics too."

"Ah yeah, about that..." My stomach sinks.

"What is it?"

"Sorry to tell you, bro, but she's a journalist. She works for the same paper that slimeball outside does. It's likely she was undercover investigating you when we met. I'm sorry - I should have cased her before inviting her on a date. Shitty security guard I am."

My head reels at the information. After keeping my secret for all these years, I've invited a journalist into my home, and she's seen me turn.

"She's not friendly with the scumbag outside though - apparently, they dated, he stole one of her stories, and she went mental on him - broke his right hand. She had to pay him to prevent him from getting a restraining order on her."

"Fits of rage fit with orc and mystic behavior," I say. "But there's definitely something wrong. It's like part of her is fighting against her natural tendencies. Did you find out anything about an anxiety disorder?"

"She had an episode when she was in high school, a similar rage attack. They diagnosed it as anxiety and put her on medication for years."

Sympathy wells in me, both for Summer and her parents. Teenage orcs are hard to control at that age when their rage is first kicking in. I don't approve of them sedating her, but I can understand why. "The medication might be affecting her mystic side. She doesn't seem aware of what she's doing when she's a mystic."

"So, you're going to do what? Ask the journalist to stop taking medication to see if she's the savior of our kind? She probably only did the ritual for a story, Tom. She won't believe she's a mystic and likely doesn't care about the orcs." Olivia's right, but it still stings when I think that Summer truly doesn't care about my people.

"What do you suggest? Assassination?"

"Or maybe since the cat's out of the bag anyway, the professor's plan? She's a journalist, right? Offer her the story. That'll get her back."

"I told you I don't want to go public." I shut the idea down instinctively. It's typical of Olivia to take any angle to push for what she wants.

"You might not have a choice. Unless you can convince her to stay quiet. At least offering her the story will secure her cooperation so you can talk about your theory about her being a mystic." Dammit, she's right.

"I don't have her number," I say.

"Got you covered, boss," my annoyingly smug sister says. I hate it when she's right. "And I'm sending some people over to your place to install some extra security measures."

I hang up unceremoniously and wait for Olivia to send me the number.

I've never been this responsive to a woman's touch, a woman's scent. I wonder if she arouses this much desire in human men and find myself growling at the thought of her with a human. A human does not deserve her sweetness.

Summer has to be convinced, consciously, that she's a mystic. Hopefully, the experiment went some way towards that, but if she feels horror or shame - my best chance at the survival of my people go with her. There's no telling if she's a full mystic, with all the famed potential of their species. She may still not be compatible with me physically. But she's given me more hope than I've had in years.

When the number comes through, I know exactly what I want to say.

CHAPTER THIRTEEN

SUMMER

Dawn is cracking the horizon as I pound the pavement, putting as much space between Tom Johnson's house and myself as possible. I'm carrying my phone in one hand and dress in the other. After two blocks I stop and take stock. I'm covered in sweat, reeking of sex, and wearing pajama sweatpants with heels.

I'm far enough away now I can call a rideshare. While I wait for it to arrive my thoughts skip around, too stressed to focus.

My thoughts keep straying to Tom's body as an orc. His breath, his scent...

I rip my thoughts away.

There have never been serious repercussions before from my fits. Steve's broken wrist was the worst thing I'd ever done - but then I've been medicated for most of my life. The last time anything like Steve had happened was when I was 14, and that was the first time I'd taken the pills that calm me down.

This morning, though - I was in full fit mode. My heart was going, I could barely think straight, and I felt an urgency fueling me. I hissed at him, for God's sake!

I remember everything that happened in Tom's bedroom, but I didn't feel like myself. I felt wanton, desperate to have him, my body on fire. And he was - I have to stop thinking about him abruptly as my body tingles at the memory.

Safer to think about what he's not. In my experience, men have been sweaty and nervous when they've been interested in me. But the orc was naked in his desire. I wanted to push him to his limit, to make him lose control completely.

The rideshare arrives and I pile into the back gratefully while my mind keeps whirring.

I think about my parents - boring, normal parents. My anxiety is a throwback, something neither of them experienced. I feel guilty they have to deal with it.

Could it really be a sign I'm a mystic? What would that even mean, that I'm not human? Does that mean Emily isn't human? But she's never suffered from my anxiety.

I'm sick to my stomach. Could we help the orc species repopulate? How would that even work? And how does this fit with my dreams of being a journalist?

I get out of the rideshare, up in the lift and roll into my apartment in a daze, barely clocking getting the key out from under the mat to unlock things. Living alone is expensive, but right now it's a godsend - not having to explain where I was or why I'm dressed like I am. The downside is that it's a shitty apartment that costs far too much, and the place is nearly empty since I just moved here.

I head straight to my bedroom, pulling fresh clothes out of a suitcase on the floor and jumping into the shower. Hot water is one of the few things this apartment has gotten right, and hopefully washing the smell of Tom off me will help clear my head.

I let the water run entirely over my head, blocking out the world and letting my muscles relax.

There's something tempting about being a mystic - the idea of being special. And maybe not just broken like I've always been told I am.

And I have to admit, there's something thrilling about being with Tom.

I block all thoughts of him from my mind for another few minutes before I get out of the shower, briskly washing my body and trying not to think of any tingling.

I'm in jeans and a t-shirt and drying my hair in my bedroom and feeling more human when I notice a message waiting on my phone. It's not a number I know.

> *Summer, I'm going with the professor's plan and want you to break my story exclusively. Come back to the apartment today. In exchange, I'd ask you to see me again before taking your next anxiety pill. I don't think you're sick - Tom*

So, he knows I'm a journalist, and that I take medication for anxiety. I'd be upset at the invasion of privacy, but I was spying on him. He doesn't even seem upset that I lied, but then he's been lying to everyone for years.

I glance at the bottle of pills next to my bed. Taking a pill was next on my list of things to do. My mother's face swims into my mind. My parents have always wanted the best for me. But maybe they were only working with half the information.

The pills make everything a bit more muted, and I've always hated them. I stopped for a while when I moved to Sydney, and I felt fine. But then the Steven incident happened. Going back on the pills reassured me something like that wouldn't happen again soon.

I'm frustrated and confused, so I do what I always do when I'm not sure what to do. I call Emily and tell her everything.

"Woah," Emily says, when I've finished my breathless rant.

"I know," I agree wholeheartedly. "You're the biologist. What do you think it means? Is it even possible?"

"It is possible that there's a recessive trait in our genes, and that your episodes result from that. Your episodes do certainly track with everything I know about orc adolescence." She's been reading since I took a job chasing orcs, out of her own curiosity. Having a nerdy sister is all kinds of handy.

"Then how do the pills work?"

"The pills might mess with your natural system. You don't really know what will happen with your new instincts without them, and they'll take a couple of weeks to leave your system. But it could be big. It could be huge for the orc species."

"Am I now responsible for the continuation of a species?"

"That I can't tell you - you might only have some traits, but not enough to breed, or to accommodate his size."

I blush down the phone at her blunt assessment. "But it's worth finding out, right?"

"I would want to know. But it's up to you. You never have to see another orc again if you don't want to. You could take this deal, get your Pulitzer, and never look back."

"If I were to test if I'm a mystic, how would it even work?..."

Emily's voice rises in volume, excited, and I know I've got her attention. "If I were you, I'd track everything - everything you eat, your emotions, your physical states, every day for the two weeks, and every reaction you have to orcs. You'd want to be somewhere quiet and safe, without too many complicating factors. Ideally, you'd run it in a controlled environment, like a proper experiment."

As she talks, I think of Tom's face, his powerful body. Then I think of the hope in his face when we were talking about the idea of the mystics, and the hurt emanating from him when we walked past his people in the alleyway.

And I think of the professor's idea - of a hero amongst the orc people, a noble king who hid his identity for years to serve his people...

"You're composing a story in your head right now, aren't you?" Emily interrupts.

Caught out, I chuckle. "Ok, you got me. Whatever Tom wants to tell me, I already know the angle I'm going to take. But it needs more research. Fortunately, I know where to get it."

I say my grateful goodbyes to Emily and call the professor.

CHAPTER FOURTEEN

TOM

I throw myself into work while waiting for Summer to get back to my message.

I find myself distracted, thinking of her, even as I let workmen into the building to install some extra security precautions Olivia insisted on.

At some point I wonder if Summer escaped the press outside without being caught. Then I catch myself - it wouldn't matter if they caught her, she's one of them. The realization sinks my stomach.

When she finally messages, I scramble for the phone.

Deal. I'll be at yours at 2pm - Summer

I check the time - it's already 1pm. But of course, she knew where I'd be. Everyone does.

I stare out the window and watch a reporter doing a tv spot across the road. The protestors aren't going away, unfortunately. There are more of them out there than earlier today. I'm not sure how Summer is going to get back in without being spotted.

I look back at the message. It's a cold message, clipped and official, and I can read nothing further into it. She owes me nothing, I remind myself. But still I feel the bitter tang of disappointment that she wants the exclusive story Olivia knew she would.

My experiences with human women so far have been anything but pleasant. My successful entrepreneur persona attracts gold diggers. They're women who don't have a real thing about them except their hunger for status.

I thought Summer was different - that she wanted to help people. Instead, she wants to expose me.

When I first learned she was a journalist, I was still reeling from our time together, but now with some space I understand what it means. She had no interest in the orc cause. I wonder about her careful words about wanting to help people with her work. Was that a lie, too? It didn't feel like it, but then I didn't know she was a journalist either.

2pm gives her time to collect herself and recover from our time together. Perhaps I need that too - to get my game face on. If she truly is a mystic, I have no choice but to get her on our side. But what will she ask in return, if we're talking about transactions? What side of her will come out now?

I forward the text exchange to Olivia, so she knows what time to expect Summer. My phone rings immediately.

"I see you've wasted no time," she says testily.

"It was a good idea, sister," I say.

"A good idea that could use a bit of a security briefing, don't you think?" she reprimands. "I told you - you should have let me hire you a publicist, and the professor will guide how this happens." She sighs loudly and I feel a touch guilty. With everything going on with Summer, I didn't think of it.

"Okay, I'm getting everyone on a video chat. We don't have time for travel," she says, and hangs up.

I brood. It's something Olivia has accused me of, and right now seems like the right time for it. I transform into my orc, because it makes me feel better, and there's no reason to stay a man now.

When the video call rings, I'm already in orc mode. The professor picks up, looking flustered. "Oh, my... Mr Tom... Mr Johnson... Olivia told me... this is certainly unexpected. It's lovely to see you in your er... natural state."

I growl deeper than I need to and enjoy the way he swallows nervously. "Well, your idea is going to come to fruition, professor. Guide me." Olivia has a notebook open and pen poised on the other line.

"Well, sir... well, as you already have an established reputation, that goes a long way towards the er... hero orc we were hoping for. You're an upstanding member of the community," he says.

"Go on," I say, when he pauses.

He lets out a sigh and continues with far less hesitation. He's clearly been waiting for this. "Ideally, you would have been involved in more charitable causes, and we will have polished your image before we let you loose in the world. And you'll have a sympathetic orc, let's say an injured orc, by your side, as an example of the disadvantaged.

"At this point really the only thing that could go wrong is being outed without your will. The public will believe you have lied to them. Summer said she was amenable to all these strategies, so you needn't worry. A sympathetic press is the key to this, and we have that."

"Summer called you?" I ask, cutting him off.

"Well, yes - she told me everything."

"Everything?" I ask, too sharply.

"Well, er..."

"What did Summer tell you exactly, professor?" Olivia says more gently than I can muster.

"Well, that she's a journalist, that Olivia figured it out, and that you revealed your secret to her and talked about enacting my publicity plan with her help. It really was brilliant of you to find such a sympathetic member of the press so quickly. And a very bright young girl."

I hang up.

Summer will not betray me - she wants to help. The crushed feeling I've been having all day lifts. And it's almost 2pm.

I change back into a man and get dressed hurriedly upstairs, wanting to be ready, unintimidating and human when she arrives. As I descend the stairs, I check out the window - the protest across the road has gotten huge, and there's a kerfuffle at one end of it.

It could be the police, and I notice the press eagerly honing in on the action. A journalist calls out to his cameraman and waves him over, but the press of agitated protesters is too thick for me to see past. The crowd moves with whatever the disturbance is, getting closer to the base of my building.

Something tells me it isn't a police officer, and before I know it, I'm ripping open my door and rushing past my startled security staff. "Wait here," I say gruffly, and know he'll get a speaking to from Olivia later when he does as I ask.

The elevator will take too long, so I look around quickly. Apart from my security man, the hallways are empty. I allow my claws to transform and swing myself over the railing, jumping down several floors to hit the bottom level. I ignore the sound of my suit jacket ripping at the shoulders.

The noise outside the door is godawful, and my heart is pounding as I approach the door. I don't stop, but retract my claws as I move. I use my security pass to exit the door and close it behind me so no reporters can sneak in.

I'm expecting to get rushed with press and protestors as soon as the door opens, but they barely notice me. They're focused on harassing Summer.

"How long have you been investigating Mr Johnson, Summer?"

"What have you found out, Summer?"

Given that she has my exclusive, I expect to find her fielding queries calmly, but she's standing stock still, eyes wide. She looks like she's ready to run - or punch in a reporter's face. She's wearing a light pink dress with a laptop backpack on.

I'm ready to rip my way through the crowd to help her when they spot me.

"Mr Johnson! What do you think of this protest, Mr Johnson?"

"What do you say about your orc assault last night, Mr Johnson?"

I keep walking through them, stepping closer to Summer. The press is difficult but tolerable.

I'm only a couple more steps. I can see her hair, catch glimpses of her face.

"How could you support these dangerous creatures?" It's the woman Olivia told me about - the one with obvious links to organized crime, shouting in my face. Beyond the woman, Summer catches my eye. She looks glad to see me and my heart leaps.

I ignore the protestor, but she stands in front of me, jamming a finger hard into my chest.

"They're nothing but animals, and you know it." Spit from her screaming flies towards me and I blink at her, distracted for a second from my goal to get to Summer.

To my left, a flash goes off as a reporter takes an opportune picture.

I'm about to push my way past them both when something stings my shoulder. I look at the dark stain blooming on my black jacket in surprise. The darkness of the fabric means that nobody else has noticed yet, but my eyes scan the crowd, looking for the shooter, who must be somewhere behind Summer.

I notice Summer's gaze land on my shoulder, her eyes widening in shock, and she spins around to look for the culprit.

I see him first, a nondescript guy in a brown trench, but she's closer. Her expression turns as vicious as any orc as she drops her backpack and lunges for him, throwing him off balance. Summer jumps on his back, clawing at him, while the shooter raises the gun up, flailing. The crowd panics, and I push the protestor to the ground and step over her to get to Summer.

The shooter shakes Summer off for a second and shoots me, point blank, twice in the chest, before turning to Summer and taking aim. That means he's not facing me when I transform into an orc. The bullets push out of my chest as I transform, just before I hit him hard across the back of the head, throwing him to the ground unconscious.

Summer leaps on him, lifting his head and slamming it into the ground. She looks wild - feral - and I wrap my orcish arms around her waist and drag her away from her prey, picking her laptop bag up as I go. Cameras click furiously around us. Fortunately, the crowd makes way.

When we reach the door of the apartment, it's a struggle to hold her with one arm and get my pass to open the door. When the green light dings to let us in, I throw her inside and follow quickly afterwards, slamming the door behind us.

For a second, I lean against the door, processing the fact that despite myself, I'm now out as an orc in the world. But I was dead if I stayed human, and there's no way I could have left Summer in trouble like that.

I turn to her, expecting her to still be on the ground where I threw her. Fortunately, inside the corridor is still deserted. There's nobody to see her throw herself on me like a wild thing, tearing at my clothes and kissing me ferociously.

CHAPTER FIFTEEN

TOM

For a moment I'm lost in her kiss. I spin to slam her into the door we just entered, welcoming her soft mouth while her legs straddle me. My hands climb up her dress to her firm thighs and grip her ass, holding her in place.

And then I remember we're on the ground floor of my apartment building, and regretfully unpeel her legs from around me, setting her down on the floor. She frowns and pouts, coming towards me again, but I hold her off. I wink. "Come and get me," I say, and take her discarded backpack with me as I leap up to catch the railing at the edge of the next floor. She tries to jump after me, and I can see the wheels turn as she remembers the elevator and runs towards it.

I swing my way up the building like King Kong while she takes the slower lift, and bark at my startled security man to stay outside and let her in. Whether he knew I was an orc, or if he'll stay, I don't really care. I head upstairs, waiting for her at the guestroom door.

My heart is pounding, the drumming of the jungle in my blood. This is the mating ritual of my kind - chase, and be chased. It's hard to think straight past the roaring in my ears.

The security guard doesn't follow her in and shuts the door after her, which is all I need. She ignores him, running towards me. I can't help but grin at the excited look in her eye as she jumps into my arms. I slam the door shut behind us and press her up against it.

Her eyes aren't red, as they would be if she was orcish, but they're wild enough. "Mystic," I say, and it's mostly growl.

She hisses at me, grinding herself against me even with her legs wrapped around my waist. She's a feral thing, too far gone to speak. I know what she needs.

I spin and I throw her on the bed, reaching for the ropes already hanging from the two curved posts at the bedhead. I tie her arms tightly and efficiently, holding her in place. If she was up to her full strength - the strength of a mystic - this wouldn't hold her.

She screeches and kicks at me, struggling against the restraints, and I lie atop her sideways, using my weight to hold her still. One arm holds her legs and the other reaches beneath her skirt, keeping my head out of reach of her snapping teeth.

One claw makes quick work of her underwear, and I rub her already soaking sex. Her back arches and she stops kicking and snapping at me, moaning in pleasure until she cries out in release.

She stills beneath me and I hold my breath. Last time we were in this position, she ran away. I lift my weight off her and look at her eyes. "Summer?" I ask tentatively.

"Yes?" she asks quietly. She looks shocked, and ashamed. I wipe my hand on the bedclothes, lower her skirt and stand up, giving her some space. She closes her legs.

"Are you okay?" I ask.

"I... I'm not sure."

"Would you like to be untied?"

She looks up at her hands, as if realising for the first time they're bound. "I... I don't think so..." her eyes well with tears. "I don't want to hurt you." She looks small and fragile suddenly. The thought of her hurting me would be ridiculous if I hadn't seen her frenzy moments ago. Hopefully she'll gain control before she reaches full strength.

"Summer." I sit on the bed and gently touch her chin and turn her face towards me until she meets my eyes. Her skin is soft and warm under my touch. "Look at me. I'm much bigger than you. I'm not afraid of you hurting me. That's not what these restraints are for. You never learned to control your orc side, so it's all coming out now, at the same time as your heat."

"Heat?" she asks. Her eyes have dried. She's still lucid. "I... stopped taking my pills. This is my anxiety condition."

"Has it ever felt like this before? With lust?" She shakes her head, eyes still on mine. My heart leaps at the trust in them. That trust is a responsibility that keeps me in control. I let her chin go, but I stay close, breathing her in. "You're acting like an orc in heat. And it's putting me in heat. The rituals we use are about trying to formalise this, to control it. But when you come after me like a wild thing, it's hard..." I stop, swallowing hard. I can't say out loud what I want to do to her.

She stares at me. "But I want you to," she says. She blushes, even as her hips shift as if of their own volition. "I can't help myself. There's something inside me, desperate for your touch." Suddenly it's hard to breath. I stand up again, ignoring the erection pressing against my shredded pants.

"Yes," I say, fists curling at my sides, facing the door away from her. "But you have options. And I want to be sure you're aware of them, while you're lucid."

I turn back to her. Her eyes are fixed on my erection. "Yes..." she says breathily. She shakes her head. "I mean no - can you even fit me, biologically?"

"If you are truly mystic, when your medication is out of your body, I'm hoping you'll be ready for me. But until then, while you can fully let go, I cannot. I will be restrained. I don't want to hurt you."

"Okay. But the medication could take weeks to leave my system. Will I be tied up the entire time?" Her legs keep shifting, rubbing against each other as she speaks. I avert my eyes, pacing the room.

"There are a few ways we can go about it. You can stay away from me and other orcs, and let the drugs leave your system. But that means we won't be able to tell how you'll react next time you see an orc."

I turn back to her. She nods, but her eyes are fixed on my crotch. My cock twitches in my pants. I close my eyes, take a deep breath and resume my pacing, further away this time. "The other option is you stay in this room until your heat ends. It's a controlled environment. Humans will bring you food and you'll be comfortable. At the end, we'll control test how you react to orcs."

Her voice is stronger and more clear now that I'm further away from her. "My sister recommended something like that. A controlled environment."

Olivia told me one of Summer's sisters is a biologist. "What your sister may not realise is your heat. It's not comfortable. Without release, you'll suffer. Normally I would recommend sedation to help you through it, but given that you're weaning off medication, it's probably a bad idea."

"So, what would you suggest?"

"The third alternative is similar to the second - you stay in this room, but with the option of release. It will help ease the symptoms of your heat and make the transition more comfortable. But the choice is yours, and you can of course change your mind at any time." I'm using my most formal voice, and can't look at her right now. My erection, now uncomfortably pressing against my zip, is doing enough to advertise which option I prefer.

By the time I bring myself to look at her, she has her eyes closed and she's breathing deeply herself. When she opens her eyes, for a second I see a tinge of red in them. "Tom Johnson," she says slowly. "While I am in full charge of my senses, I'd like to remind you that you owe me a story. I expect a full interview, regardless of which option I choose."

I blink. That's not what I expected to hear, but she's speaking clearly, in the language of negotiations, and that makes me very comfortable. "Agreed."

"In that case, I choose door number three. And I'm in need of release right now."

Chapter Sixteen
SUMMER

I hold my breath, waiting for Tom's response to my invitation. Something inside me is close to exploding. While Tom's been pacing, I can feel the hunger inside me pushing against my senses, and it's all I can do to form a coherent sentence. He starts towards me and a moan escapes my lips. The release he gave me earlier wasn't nearly enough to satisfy me.

And then he's right there beside me, on the bed, huge and on top of me. His hot breath mingles with mine in a fierce kiss as he clenches my wrists beneath their bounds. I smile into his kiss, enjoying the press of him, and the rising heat in my body at having him so close. His touch is like fuel to the flames inside me.

He sits up beside me on the bed, and starts untying my bonds. Through the haze of lust scoring through me, I hesitate. "Wait..." The image of Steve clutching his broken arm comes to me. "I can't control it." I'm panting now, my vision blurring, my voice slurring.

Tom keeps untying, not looking at me, his orc fingers surprisingly deft with the knots. One of my hands releases. "You don't need to control yourself, Mystic," he says. "That's my job."

Before I can object further, his hand is on my throat, pinning me to the bed. The force inside me swells in response to the challenge and I'm kicking, clawing and hissing at him, indignant at his attempts to tame me. I can see and hear everything, but I couldn't speak now if I tried. Something else has hold of me.

With one hand, he easily bats aside my arms and rips a claw down my front, ripping my dress straight down the middle. He pauses, admiring the view. "You are majestic," he says. "But if I rut you now, Mystic, I will tear you in two, and neither of us will have the sense to stop me. Fortunately there are other ways to release."

He claws off his pants with his free hand, then releases my throat only to grab the back of my hair and push my mouth towards his free erection. He uses one hand to pleasure himself, rubbing the end of his cock against my mouth. The salty taste speaks to the wild thing inside me. Soon I'm biting and sucking hard, taking as much of him as I can - more than I ever have with a man before - until he explodes down my throat. I swallow it down hungrily. He releases his hold on my hair.

The taste of him brings some of my senses back. "Tom," I croak, but his hand is around my neck again, and I'm slammed back onto the bed. His thick fingers slide readily inside my wetness while his tongue laps at my breasts, and soon my legs are shaking in an earth-shattering release.

He releases my neck and collapses onto the bed next to me. My legs are still jelly when I feel him roll off the bed. A pang of anxiety spikes in my chest - is he leaving already?

Instead he turns back into a man. His body is smaller, but he's still well-built. I find myself staring until he scoops me up and carries me, bridal-style, into the bathroom, and sets me down on the sink while he turns the shower taps on. "While you're still lucid," he says, "We should take the opportunity to clean up." He gestures me into the shower and I follow instructions. "And while you're feeling compliant," he says ruefully, and steps in beside me.

There's enough room in the extra large shower for both of us. I don't speak while he applies lather to his hands and rubs down my body. He doesn't slow down around my breasts. His movements are gentle, but efficient. His hands feel good - caring. I get the impression he really is moving fast to make the most of the time. Which worries me. "How long will I be in heat?" I ask.

"It's hard to tell. The legends say continually for two weeks, but there must be respites to eat and sleep," he says, moving me into the shower to rinse off. When he's satisfied he moves me out again, and applies shampoo to my hair. I let him. It feels incredible, and I close my eyes while he continues. "You don't have to worry about a thing. The fridge is fully stocked. I'll make sure you eat properly."

And now it feels weird. He moves me so the lather rinses out of my hair. I rub water out of my eyes. "I'm not a child," I say, irritably. "And I haven't forgotten you owe me a story."

He steps back and begins to wash himself while I condition my own hair. "The change also comes with some moods," he says, amused. I resist the urge to stick my tongue out at him.

"When do I get my interview?" I say.

"You can interview me any time you like. We'll be together for long enough, after all." He makes it sound like a duty. I rinse off the conditioner and step out of the shower, reaching for one of the soft, fluffy bathrobes that are waiting on a hook behind the door.

He's right - my moods are zinging all over the place. I was irritable a moment ago, and now I've stepped away from him I feel vulnerable. We've been intimate, but I know almost nothing about him.

"Okay then, what is it you miss the most about your home world?" I ask, turning to face him in the shower. He's washing his hair now. The way his arms are lifted make his biceps stand out. The fire inside me perks up. Apparently even his human form is doing it for me now. I push my libido down to listen to his response.

"I miss hunting the *shianas* - something like deer on your world - and the nights around the fire when the fighting was quiet. But we were always slaves - serving one army or another. For hundreds of years. Even though we're dying here, we're still free. That's why I have to make it work - make a home for us here." He sounds tired.

"It must be difficult, having to hide all the time, with the pressure of leadership."

"I was raised to leadership," he says. "But yes, I worry about my people. I worry about our future." He turns the taps off and grabs his own robe. His voice is hard now, the billionaire back and the orc who threw me on the bed gone. He walks back into the bedroom, and I follow.

"I hope I can help," I say. "In a few weeks we'll know. And if I'm not a mystic, I'll be out of your life forever." When I say it out loud, I realize it's something I've been afraid to voice.

He turns and looks at me, and the sharpness of the predator is back in his eyes. His gaze pins me in place. "I know you're not helping me for a book deal," he says. "We haven't been very honest with each other until now, and that's on both of us. But when you told me you wanted to help people... even though you were lying about being an intern, it felt true. I think that's why you're here."

I nod, swallowing. There's something about it, when he looks at me like this. Like he's really seeing me - not as the hope of his people, or a mystic, but as me. He steps towards me, and my body perks up. But I want to keep him like this, seeing me, for a little longer.

So I start blathering, the words bypassing my brain. "When I first got to Sydney, I trusted another journalist, and I shouldn't have. I was researching a story on street kids in my own time. It was going to be my big story - the one that impressed my editor. They were minors, but they didn't want to go back into the system. There was no way I could write the story without sacrificing their freedom, and it had taken me months to earn their trust. In the end, I just couldn't do it. But then I told Steve..."

"And he broke the story." His eyes snap, his mouth a hard line. I hope for Steve's sake he never meets Tom.

"Yes. He stole my notes. It forced the authorities to crack down and chase up the minors. The kids went back in, and

Steve - he said I'd compromised my journalistic ethics, that I'd never cut it. He thought he did the right thing. And of course, his career benefited."

Tom makes a noise - a cynical hmph. He's standing right in front of me now, close enough to touch. His eyes are still on mine.

"But I thought maybe he's right. I can't seem to separate myself from the story, even now..." I laugh nervously. "I felt so guilty lying to you about who I was. Maybe I'm not meant to be a journalist."

"Well, you broke my story," he says wryly. He reaches out a hand to push a strand of hair behind my ear.

"That was an accident," I confess. While he's been talking, the heat in my body has been slowly rising, and my breathing has become more shallow. I know he can see it.

He steps closer towards me and speaks into my ear while he undoes the tie of my robe. "Summer. You stuck to your own values. That's worth more than any career, and shows far more integrity than it sounds like this Steve has," His voice is firm. Although he's far from an orc, he's different from the cold billionaire I met in the professor's offices. "You're a fierce woman with good instincts. I think you haven't heard that enough."

He runs his hands over my shoulders, pushing the robe onto the floor. I swallow hard. "I know you're not as vulnerable as you appear, but sometimes that's hard to see," he says, and his eyes drop now, roaming my naked body. He places his hands around my waist and walks around me, his hands trailing me until he's out of my view.

The air behind me shifts. A hot tongue licks my ear. Tom's deep orcish voice says, "What do your instincts say now, Summer?"

I run.

Chapter Seventeen

SUMMER

I run, and feel the thrill of the monster chasing me. I slam the bedroom door behind me. It almost catches him as I fly ahead. He snarls behind me, and calls out. I'm dimly aware there are rules to this game, but blood is rushing in my ears and all I can think of is the chase as I leave the apartment behind.

The inside of the warehouse soars above me, but he is right behind me, and he's angry - I can feel it, hear it in his roars. He could tear me in two. He can try! I laugh and stand on the railing of this floor, jumping to the floor below. I land hard and roll. It hurts. He lands beside me easily. I roll away, get up and run.

His arm is around my waist - catching me, too fast. The chase is over too soon! I kick and scream and he lets go. It's on again! He yells after me and I run into the glass box that will take me up, pressing the button to close the doors. He can't get me here.

The doors are closing when his claw gets in the way. Fear zips through me. It's only a game, yes? But he's very big. He roars again as he pries the doors open. The glass of the small box shakes.

Behind him, a human sticks their head out of their apartment door and then shuts it again. They look afraid. He is scary, but I'm ready for him. I leap on him as he enters the box, hissing. He throws me back against the wall as the elevator shuts behind him.

"Mystic, while I enjoy our games, there are rules you must obey," he says, stepping towards me. I snarl at him and swipe my nails across his chest. They don't make a dent. I keep swiping and kick out at him with my feet. He steps towards me again, pressing me into the glass wall behind me. "Until you are strong enough to become a predator, in our games you will be prey." He grabs my shoulder and twists me around, pressing my naked body into the cold glass. He holds my wrists behind me with one hand and slips another between my legs, rubbing at the moist nub there until I cry out.

My head clears. "Tom…"

"You are coming back to yourself?" He asks.

"Yes," I say, expecting him to let me go. Instead he dips a finger inside my wetness, making my knees go weak. I whimper at the pleasure of it. From here, I can see the row of apartment doors as the elevator goes up. A man opens his front door as the elevator passes his floor. He sees us, his eyes widen, and he shuts the door again. Shame spikes through me.

"Tom, I'm okay now. I don't need..." I groan as he shifts his finger slowly inside me. We pass another floor. Any moment now, someone else might open their apartment door and see us. I wiggle against him. My nipples are hard against the glass, enhancing the pleasure. "More people might see us," I gasp.

"Good. Your mystic doesn't understand punishment, but you do. This is your punishment for leaving the apartment." His finger pumps inside me, relentless. "I'll have a lock installed tomorrow so it won't happen again. But when you run like this, you test my control," he says, and he presses another finger inside me. I gasp. It's so full! I squirm against his hand. "I can feel that you're not ready yet to take my cock, are you, Mystic?" I shake my head against the glass, afraid that if he moves too fast he'll hurt me. But he goes slowly - slowly and steadily. Pleasure builds inside me, and I whimper. We pass another floor, then hit the top. The elevator doors open, but I barely notice as I cry out in a release so strong it makes my womb ache, my sex clenching against his fingers.

In the hazy aftermath of the release, my head becomes light, and my eyes roll back as I whisper, *"Divided blood will flow."* It barely sounds like my voice, and I didn't shape the words consciously, but I know they're true.

Tom lets my arms go, grabs my shoulder and turns me around, hand on my chin. "Summer?" His gaze is worried, searching my eyes. I lean my head into his shoulder, letting him hold me, and processing.

I made a prediction. It's almost too much - too much responsibility, and too much of a shift from the pleasure and shame I was feeling only moments ago.

It feels good to be held in his arms. It feels safe here.

I think about what we've just done, in a glass elevator for the world to see. The shame stings, but my body is still singing. And my blood runs hot - with lust, yes - my mystic can't get enough - but also freedom.

For so long I've been worried about what I might do, who I might hurt, with my rage. Tom promises to tame the wildness inside me. And even his punishments are pleasure. With him, I don't need to restrain myself. I don't need to hold back. I'm done playing it safe.

I pull my head back again to meet his eyes. "That was a prediction, Tom. A true one."

"Thank you, my Mystic," he says reverently, and takes my hand and kisses it. His eyes stay on mine, uncertain what happens next.

"You'd better buy a strong lock, orc," I say, defiant, with a feral grin, and push him off me.

He grins back, sensing the game. He grabs me and kisses me fiercely, his erect cock pressed hard against my stomach. "In that case, your punishment continues," he says, and presses me back until my ass hits the glass. Grabbing the back of my head, he forces my mouth down onto his cock while he kicks my feet open. He pushes against me, pressing my sex into the wall of the glass elevator, putting me on full display for the apartment doors around us. "Fortunately for me, there are enough floors left to show this building what a good girl you can be." He reaches behind him and presses all the buttons. The elevator will stop at every floor and the doors will open.

By the time Tom carries me back into his apartment, I'm ready for my next release.

Chapter Eighteen

TOM

I answer the phone to my irritating sister. "It's Olivia," I explain to Summer. She's tied to the bed, naked. I'm in my orc body, also naked, kneeling above her, the phone in my hand.

"Hi Summer!" Olivia calls out through the phone. "Sorry to interrupt. Just wanted to check in, really. See how things are progressing."

My nostrils flare in irritation, but my sister is entitled to check in. She's taking progress back to our people, and it's been three weeks. Summer's medication could wear off completely any day now, and they're obviously very invested in how things are going.

I look apologetically at Summer and reach out to untie one of her hands. She shakes her head. "Be quick," she mouths, and tips her chin at the door, telling me to get out and make my phonecall brief. I nod and jog into the hallway to give Olivia the update.

Summer likes Olivia, although my sister's timing is terrible. Olivia somehow found magic dealers on Earth. She gave us a potion to help us sleep, and a salve to help us with chafing. If not for that, the heat would have kept Summer and I up all night, and we would rub ourselves raw.

"Things are progressing well here. And you?" I say to Olivia. I'm terse, but I'm still thinking of Summer on the bed. I walk to the stairway and sit at the top landing, enjoying the feel of the morning sunlight on my bare green flesh. From here I can see the throws on the couch are a crumpled mess - evidence of the activities of the house for the past two weeks.

I don't bother shifting to human or wearing clothes anymore. Summer's scent is embedded through the entire apartment, so if I try to sleep human I inevitably revert back to an orc.

"Ten more orcs turned up at our facility," Olivia says. It's a good sign. Summer's mere existence is bringing more orcs over to my way of thinking, luring them away from my brother's bad influence. She's brought hope. She's made them believe in me. "But they want word of the mystic. I hear Summer has a book offer," Olivia says.

I huff down the phone. "She has several. She's playing them off against each other," I say approvingly. We have had occasional down patches when the heat eases off. Not many, but I've found them almost as enjoyable as the sex.

"I do like her blog posts, although they haven't been very frequent," she adds.

"Olivia, get to the point, I'm busy, and I know what you've called for. No, Summer hasn't shown any more orcish traits, no she hasn't had any more predictions. No, I don't know any more what her prediction means. You will be the first to know if anything happens. And I'm assuming there's been no movement with our brother." I glance behind me at the open doorway to Summer's room, then I stand up and walk down the stairs, just in case. I asked Olivia to check in on Evan after Summer's prediction.

Apparently he's been doing what he's been doing for his entire time on Earth, patching together small jobs, barely making ends meet, and convincing other orcs not to follow me. He's a huge pain in my ass, but so far he hasn't proven to be any more than that. If it weren't for Summer's prediction, I wouldn't give him much thought right now.

"No movement on Evan," Olivia confirms. Then she says what's obviously been on her mind. "What if Summer's not a full mystic, Tom? She might not be able to breed with you. Have you thought about how you'll handle that? With her – and with our people?" I try to ignore the stomach flip of anxiety at her words. I've been trying very hard not to think about that.

I stare out the window at the military ship in port below. There are no men on it right now, so it's just a flat grey landscape of metal and rigging.

"I know it's not a done deal, Olivia. I just... mystic or not..." I struggle to continue. I won't give Summer up. It's something I've known in my heart for some days now. For years, my people have come first. But now, I want something for myself. "If Summer isn't a full mystic, I know it's my duty to keep looking for one to breed with...." I say out loud.

Before I can continue, Summer crashes into me from behind, snarling. The phone is flung from my hand and I throw my arms around up to ward off her claws - claws? Her eyes are red, her skin tinted purple, and she's stronger than I remember. Strong enough to break out of the ropes on the bed, I realise. She's still got a piece of rope tied to one arm.

I throw her down on the couch, but she's up before I can grab her, running to the door. Fortunately, I've had it locked, and I laugh when she turns and hisses at me. I stop laughing when she grabs a knife from the kitchen block.

She lunges at me, swiping, and I dodge out of the way and grab a couch cushion to hold in front of me. "You are mine, orc," she hisses, and I'm shocked she can speak. Shocked enough not to block the next swipe. My chest stings from the deep cut, red blood freely running down my chest.

When she swipes again I use the pillow to pin her arms together and swing her body into the glass wall. It shudders but doesn't crack. It's reinforced, but may not withstand the intensity of an orc mating ritual.

She's dazed enough to drop the knife, and I grab her neck, trying to push her down to the ground. Instead she leaps around and attaches herself behind my neck, choking me with the rope still attached to her arm.

If I pass out, I can't control what happens. Will I still have an erection? She could impale herself on it regardless of whether her body can take me. We can't both be out of control.

Black dots dance in my vision while I spin around and slam her again into the glass. It cracks. She holds on tight. I slam her back again, too far from a wall for anything else to be useful. She holds on, and we fall backwards into space.

I slam into the metal floor. It wakes me up with sudden pain. I gasp and try to sit up. Summer is beside me, already getting to her feet. If she runs, I might not catch her.

I lunge for her, pushing her down on the deck on her back and pressing my body on top of hers. It hurts but it's worth it. We end up splayed on the deck top to tail, with me on top. My blood is sticky between us. She writhes beneath me and I can't resist her wild scent. I'm close enough to lap at her sex with my tongue, and her screeches turn to moans beneath me.

Fresh liquid floods my tongue. It tastes like her, but with a twist of fresh jasmine. A shudder runs through me. My sore muscles relax, no longer strained against pain. I suck harder, taking more of her in. My pain ebbs further. Realisation dawns - in this form, her fluids are healing. A rare and unexpected talent for a mystic.

She softens, opening her legs for me so I can properly attend to her clitoris. My fingers explore her, testing the stretch of her new form. She can take two fingers with ease.

She gasps underneath me. "Tom," she says. I'm surprised again - she hasn't released yet, but is talking. It's a good sign.

"Yes?" I lift my body off her, bracing myself with one hand while the other keeps up its explorations inside her.

"Are you mine, orc?" She doesn't ask the question with insecurity - but with challenge. I look at her properly. Stretched beneath me, I can appreciate how beautiful she is in her new form. She still looks like Summer, but somehow enhanced.

I can easily say out loud now what I hesitated to say to Olivia. "Yes, Mystic, I am yours. Only yours."

I press another finger inside her. Her eyes roll back in her head and her back arches, but she takes my fingers easily. Her whole body shudders with her release. "And you are mine."

I push myself up, pull my fingers from inside her and push them into her waiting mouth, letting her suck her own juices. Her eyes open wide so I explain gently about her healing juices. I encourage her to drink, plunging my fingers alternating between her pussy and her mouth until she gasps again and stops me with a hand. Her eye and then her mouth are on my ready cock.

My eyes roll up and close as she works, but I'm distracted by our location and I soon open them again.

It's early in the morning and most of the restaurants that line the wharf are closed. There are very few humans walking around, and the ship is too high for most of them to see us, even if they are on the wharf. I look for the press, however. I don't give a damn, but she might feel differently when the heat fades.

There are no cameras, but across the street, under the shadows of a building, a bulky form in a grey jacket watches us. He's wearing a hood so I can't see his face, but he's big enough to be an orc, and he's looking right at us. I sit up, gently pushing Summer off me, and he turns to leave. From here, I can see he's missing a hand. Evan. A chill runs through me.

Summer follows my line of sight and raises an eyebrow at me in question. "We have to go," is all the explanation I can offer right now. I will tell her everything eventually, but first we have to get inside.

We get into the apartment fast - with us both in our strong orcish forms, we climb back into the building.

While we climb, I wonder what trouble my brother will bring. We were once close, but he's furious at how integrated I am with the humans. His missing hand means he can't turn, and it frustrates him. He says the work I do isn't orcish. He was never so provincial in our homeland. But he can't do much more damage than he's already done, splitting our people and preventing me from helping them.

When we get back into the apartment I have other things to think about. Two panels from the glass wall are completely gone. I call Olivia, who says she'll sort it out. When I get off the phone, Summer's still in her orc form. She takes a shower to try the focusing technique I use to change forms. I throw on a robe but don't bother with the shower.

While she's gone, the doorbell rings. It's tradespeople arriving to fit out fresh glass. Nothing like money, and a sister with enough foresight to know we'd break the glass at some point.

While the tradespeople are in the apartment, I stay downstairs, on the couch, as they move around me. I get lost in my phone, catching up on the emails I've been behind for the past three weeks. Soon after come the cleaners. Olivia didn't ask, but knew they'd be needed.

Two hours later, everyone is gone, the apartment is spotless and I've made a dent in my emails. I'm still on the couch, but at some point I made a phonecall to my accountant and changed into human form. My identity may be public but that doesn't mean my orc form makes people comfortable.

Summer walks down to the base of the stairs, fully human, in one of Olivia's t-shirts and sweatpants. "I think I'm out of heat," she says with a half smile. She's right. Neither of us have been this long without each other in the past three weeks. And I'm thinking about work again, not to mention a nagging worry about my brother.

She folds her arms around herself. I know what she's thinking. We still haven't had penetrative sex. There's no telling whether she's a full mystic, or whether we're compatible, even though all signs point to yes. And what are we when we're not ripping each other's clothes off?

"Of course," I say, as I walk towards her. "The timing is good - it looks like you're definitely a mystic, and the medication is out of your system." I want to wrap my arms around her, to show her how I feel.

But as I reach her, she straightens her back and looks up at me. "Are you still mine in this form, orc?" she asks.

I smile down at her. "Yes, my mystic," I say, and take her hands in mine.

"Then I'd like to cook for you tonight, before we do the full ritual." I like that she no longer blushes when she says things like that. She stands on her tiptoes and kisses me lightly. I embrace her, loving the feel of her in my arms and trying to ignore the buzz of tension in the back of my mind.

Right now, we're perfect, and she's my queen. Right now, we have the hope of the world before us. I'll be ignoring Olivia's calls until after tonight. If Summer and I are incompatible, I will eventually have to face my sister. I'll have to face all my people. Whatever happens tonight will determine if I remain their king.

Chapter Nineteen

SUMMER

My hand shakes on the wooden spoon when I hear the key in the lock, but I steady it.

I'm wearing the black dress I was wearing on the date I went on with Tom three weeks ago, and an off-white apron over it.

Tom's no longer crazed with my heat, and he was distant and crotchety for the rest of the day, so I sent him off to work. I know he doesn't tell me everything about the orcs, and I know leadership weighs on him. He hasn't said anything, but I wonder how worried he is about tonight.

I keep my hand stirring the pot as he enters.

"Mm - smells delicious," Tom says, entering in his human guise. He's holding a bottle of wine. He seems relaxed, but his smile is tighter than normal.

"It's a curry," I say.

He steps up behind me, close but not enough to touch. My body tingles. The electricity of having him close is softer than it used to be – warmer. Tonight there's an extra edge of anticipation. My heart races, but I'm not afraid. I know I can do this.

"Did you want to pour the wine? I'll serve up." I turn the stove off and take a deep breath, avoiding his gaze as we navigate around each other.

We eat calmly, politely, despite the fire burning through my veins at having him near. Tension sits thickly in the air. I wish it were only passion. But the lines of his shoulders and the crinkle in his brow speak otherwise. He's anxious about tonight.

After we finish I clear my throat and address the issue head on. "I know we don't know if we're... compatible... and that's the whole point of this, isn't it? The potential preservation of your species?"

He nods, expression grave. He reaches out to clasp his hands around mine. My heart beats faster at his touch. His eyes have me pinned with the intensity I expect from Tom, but with a softness that didn't used to be there. "Even if we're not compatible, I have no intention of ending this. We'll get through it together." I nod, blinking back sudden tears of relief.

"Okay then," He clears his throat, and leans back, suddenly the businessman again. "I have some things prepared for a full ritual. To make it official."

I love the businessman in him. I grin and put out my hand. He takes it and shakes it like a business deal.

His expression turns mischievous and, keeping his eyes trained on me, he turns my hand over and licks it. My breath catches, electricity running from his tongue right down to my core. "You still smell delicious," he says. Then he goes back to drinking his wine.

I take a drink of my own, grateful that the glass stays steady.

When we're both finished, he raises his eyebrows and says, "shall we?" If I didn't know him well, I wouldn't notice the tension he still carries, that he's trying so hard to hide.

But who am I kidding? I'm right there with him. No matter what his intentions are, Tom's people mean everything to him. How long will we last if I turn from their great hope to their biggest disappointment?

I hope none of this shows on my face as I nod, mouth dry.

He takes my hand and walks me into his room. It smells musty, and distinctly like Tom. We've been in a million different positions in every room in the house except this one. It feels significant. I haven't been in here since our first experiment.

Like the last time we were in here, he carefully disrobes, placing all his human things away. Then his orc bursts out.

My breath catches, and for a second all thoughts leave me except his naked flesh. Will I ever get used to the sight of him? Nothing has felt more right than this.

He reaches a big green hand into his closet and hands me a sheer dress on a hanger. "Dress for me, Mystic," he grumbles in his low register.

I swallow and slip out of my dress, letting it pool to the ground at my feet. His hooded eyes watch me. His cock is hard and huge, but he doesn't touch himself.

I strip out of my bra and step out of my underwear, then slip the transparent sheath on. It's more erotic than being naked - my nipples pull against the fabric - they feel good. My heart is beating fast, and I'm wet between my legs, but I feel in control. My body is still human. Tom stays where he is, watching me, waiting for me to finish dressing.

With his eyes on me, I forget my fears. I forget everything but him.

"On the bed," he says.

I sit on the edge of the bed, and he leans down to kiss me on the lips. It's a gentle gesture, and I crane up to him, enjoying the tenderness and the flutter it brings to my stomach before I feel his claws on my hips.

Then I'm lifted in to the air and placed back down further up the bed. He slides his enormous hands up my thighs slowly, sliding the fabric up with them. When the fabric is pooled at my ass, he spreads my legs and leans down.

He hooks his arms under my thighs, and his hot breath hits my most sensitive places.

When his tongue touches me I cry out - his tongue is so hot, so thick, so wet and strong, pressing against me right where I need it. But this time I'm in control, and I could stop - I just don't want to. This is the freedom he gives me – the freedom to let go. I come in seconds, a fresh wetness flooding me.

My body shifts - I feel it growing larger, my mystic body adding muscle, fangs and a purple tinge to my skin. My senses sharpen, and I whimper at the soft press of his claws on my thighs.

"A fine dessert for your fine meal," he says.

I snort and look down at him. Tom Johnson as an orc is grinning up at me. I laugh out loud, then gasp as he laps at me again, his tongue more insistent this time, licking me from anus to clitoris in long laps. Pleasure mounts inside me again.

He chuckles and gently unhooks his arms from under my thighs and sits back. From here I can see the full length and breadth of his body, and his very hard, very large erection. I catch my breath at the sight, and the fear I'd forgotten rises again. I'm still not sure I can take that thing inside me. Will he want me if we're incompatible?

Before my nerves can take that thought any further, he gently strokes my clitoris with his claw - the pressure feels good and I let my head roll back.

He pushes a finger inside me and I whimper. He gently pumps his finger in and out, using his thumb to lazily circle my swollen nub. My muscles clench and contract into another orgasm and I cry out.

He slips another finger inside me, and my body stretches easily for him.

It feels incredible, as does the fixated expression on his face as he watches me. He may be invested in sex for the survival of his species, but this moment is just for us. In this moment his eyes convince me more than his words ever could that he will stay with me, whatever happens. That he loves me.

Finger gently pumping inside me, he tucks his arms under my thighs again and laps at my sex. My body sings.

"Sit up," he says, voice strained, and I do so, dazed.

It's a thrilling sensation to be effortlessly lifted off the bed and placed into the big orc's lap, straddling him. He puts his hands on my butt-cheeks and hoists me closer. My core is dripping wet and pressing against the length of his hard cock.

I gasp, wondering if he's going to impale me right now. My body craves him, but I have my full senses now, and I know enough to be scared. Scared of what might happen if we don't fit. Scared of the pain immediately and of the consequences later.

Would he really give everything up for me? And would I really let him?

He stops, leans forward and kisses me gently on the mouth. It's wider than a normal human mouth, but soft. His hands knead my ass, claws lightly playing with me, until he pulls away. I'm twisting in his lap now, pressing myself against his cock, when he pulls back and sets me down.

He gently pulls down the straps of the mystic's robe, pinning my arms in place as he leans forward and licks and sucks on my nipples. I should feel caught, but I feel safe in his arms, in his gentleness.

"I thought the stories of mystics in this world were a myth. They're fairy tales - like men falling asleep in fields and returning three years later."

He kisses my mouth softly before returning to my breasts, telling his story as he goes. "Mystics can look human, but can never truly be satisfied by a human mate." His voice grows deeper at his last words. "Would you like me to satisfy you, Summer?"

We can't delay any longer. My core aches with the need for him, even as my soul cries for what could be our last moment of perfection. But whatever happens, I have to know. We have to know. "Yes."

He drops his hands to my butt-cheeks again, lifting me up and lowering me onto the head of his cock, holding me there while he nuzzles my breasts.

"Do you want more?"

"Yes," I gasp, and he lowers me a centimeter. My body stretches - it hurts, but not sharply. Like a burn. And under that burn, pleasure. It's working! Hope blooms in my chest and I laugh out loud and writhe in his arms, wanting more. But he holds me firmly in place. He won't give me more until I ask. "More, please."

He lowers me a centimeter further. "More," I pant. It hurts more now. But I won't stop.

His head is away from my breasts now - his breath hot on my face as he looks at me intensely. His eyes are liquid fire - the savage beast I wanted more than I knew - and beneath his lust, a tenderness, and a relief that echoes my own. He would have stayed with me even if this didn't work. Even if I couldn't be the queen he wanted. Which makes me want to give him everything.

"More," I say, gaze locked with his.

He lowers me further, and I groan deeply, feeling a shudder in my core at the fullness. The ache is still there. He growls - low in his chest, a rumble that runs right through him.

I can feel the skin connect and know he's right inside me. I wrap my arms around his neck to lift and lower myself in a slow and steady rhythm. The ache gives way to pleasure, always shivering on the edge of pain, but never quite reaching it as I relax around him.

He groans deeply. "Summer" he says, voice betraying a need and vulnerability that pangs strangely in my chest. A thrill runs through me as my pleasure rises - it echoes the madness I used to feel, the pride and savagery, that I feel triumph at this enormous creature, humbled by me.

"Come for me," I say.

He brings his eyes back to me again, hawk-like gaze intense upon me. "You first." He grabs my hips, lifting my body easily up and down, plunging into me over and over again. I laugh aloud again – in joy, in relief, in pleasure, until he has me gasping.

When my body finally shudders in release, the orgasm is so intense it feels like a cramp. My whole body seizes and squeezes around him, not wanting to let him go.

My head feels light, and I float on pleasure while he roars so loudly it shakes the windows.

My eyes roll back and I hear myself whisper sibilantly, *"The tangled witch will unite the people."*

I collapse onto him with a sigh, and he gently kisses my forehead and lays me back down on the bed, and him down beside me. He wraps one arm around me and tugs me close. I feel boneless - I've never felt this relaxed and satiated on every level. He is mine, I am his.

But I heard my own prediction, and it came with images this time - an image of the brother Tom hasn't mentioned to me yet. I frown into his chest. I'm done with the secrets. Now I'm his queen, I will know everything before the week is done. But right now I can't bring myself to destroy the moment.

The last thing I hear before I slip into unconsciousness is him whispering into my ear, "Summer." My exhausted body feels warm when he growls my name. "You are orcish, my mystic queen, and you are mine."

Love this book?

Sign up to my newsletter and <u>get the epilogue for FREE.</u>

FREE BOOK

<u>Claim your free copy of Taming the office orc</u>. It's about a shy witch who can't do magic, a charismatic orc making his own way in the human world, and the sparks that fly when they meet.

You can claim the story, and find out more about me at
authorlamonteiro.com
Or @AuthorLAMonteiro on Instagram, TikTok and Facebook.

WHAT NEXT?

The next book in the Seasonal Spice Series is the first book about witches....

Bound by the Mages

Cassia frowns in concentration at the cauldron on her stove. Bright pink liquid bubbles inside it. *So far so good.* Symphonic metal screams from the speaker beside her, but she barely hears it.

Steel bowls lie scattered around her on a vintage-look kitchen counter, and she holds a vial of red flower petals in her hand.

She tips the vial above the cauldron and taps it gently with her finger. Petals float down towards the surface. *One... Two...*

The pounding at the door shakes the room. The bowls around her clank together. Her hand shakes, and two more petals fall into the cauldron. The bubbling pink liquid turns brown.

Shit.

She slams the vial down and flicks off the speaker next to her. It's wired through the house, not just this room. Silence falls abruptly. She storms down the corridor towards the door, past half-painted walls and a ladder she keeps meaning to move. The floorboards are streaked with scratches.

The glass panel strips on the front door are rattling from the knocking. It's an old house, and the knocking could crack the glass. *What kind of arrogant asshole...*

She throws the door open, hands on hips, ready to confront whoever interrupted her spell.

Her heart leaps in her chest.

It's one of the mage brothers who moved next door. Not the sexy one with the motorbike and the mess of dark hair. The other one, who looks as stiff as a lawyer representing a high class client in court.

He's still pretty, she has to admit. His hair is artfully arranged atop his head in a modern cut, short on the sides and back. Coiffed designer stubble offsets his square jaw. He's wearing a suit with an old-fashioned blue cravat, even though he can't be older than she is - around 30 to her 25. The cravat is almost a bow - like a gift.

Special delivery. And way hotter than my infuriating ex Darren.

The thought is an unwelcome intrusion. She's not thinking about Darren and his effortless charm and pretty face. If she thinks about him, then she thinks about what he did to her. From there, her thoughts go to the mess in the kitchen and what it means for her business and her life. Better to focus on the pretty boy in front of her, who ruined her potion.

"What do you want?" she snaps.

"For a start, you could turn the music down," he says, blue eyes icy under furrowed brows. There's an arrogant glint in his eye. Of course, there is - he's a mage. They think they're the only magic users who matter.

"It's 6pm," she points out.

He arches a single eyebrow. "So?"

"So, it's not a late hour. No other neighbors have complained." She doesn't add that a 'don't notice me' spell doubles as a noise blocker to non-magic users. Her only other magically inclined neighbor, Mrs Maisley, is a doddery old witch with poor hearing.

He's unmoved. "I'm complaining now."

"If you don't like the noise, maybe you shouldn't have moved in."

He stares her down. Her eyes meet his with equal challenge. She hates entitled men most of all. His beauty makes him even more irritating.

Although his gaze doesn't waver, eventually he clears his throat and speaks in a clipped tone. "My name is Lincoln West, and I recently moved in next door with my brother, Bradley. Although we were aware there were witches in the area, we didn't think it would be an issue to have neighbors who want to play with magic. We're respectful people. I expect the same courtesy."

His eyes drift past her. The door to the front bedroom is ajar. It's layered in drop cloths, paint cans and other signs of an abandoned renovation. She bristles, feeling his judgment from his shiny shoes to his coiffed hair.

It doesn't help that her hair's a rat's nest, kept in place in a loose bun atop her head. She's wearing her oldest black cotton dress and an apron splattered in old potions. And she barely slept last night trying to get this spell right. She looks awful. She feels awful. And his nose is pointed up like she's something scraped off his shoe.

She folds her arms.

"Well, Mr West, my name is Cassia Theseira, and I think it's just like a mage to expect the world to bend to them.

Just because mages specialize in one kind of magic and don't use spells doesn't make you better than witches. And I was in Oakford first, Lincoln, so don't expect me to change my lifestyle because I have new neighbors. If you don't like it, you can call the police and make a noise complaint. Good luck with that." She slams the door in his face.

Read more in <u>Bound by the Mages</u>

THANKS

A lot of people contributed to the creation of this book.

In short:

Enormous thanks to all of the beta readers, mentors, and fellow writers from the many writing groups I've been a part of on my writing journey. Couldn't have gotten this far without the inspiration and sympathetic camaraderie.

The long list:

Peter Cowan Writers Centre fellows from the Four Centres Emerging Writers Program

Stephen Dedman for mentoring support through the Four Centres program

The Katharine Susannah Prichard Fantasy, SciFi and Horror writing group (FISH)

Soulmate writers group

Writing on the Moon writers group

Romance Writers Australia

www.ingramcontent.com/pod-product-compliance
Lightning Source LLC
Chambersburg PA
CBHW070321120726
47909CB00008B/2545